KU-531-013

"I know one other thing. I'm not going to wait another fifteen years before I kiss you again."

His mouth settled on hers. His lips were soft and warm and inviting. As sweet as a first kiss. But then everything changed and the boy in her mind became a fully grown version of the person she'd loved. His mouth ravaged hers, exploring, igniting a young girl's passion into a woman's need. The sensation of being devoured by that hot, hungry kiss tingled through her body and she answered it with equal passion. It was like coming home and finding a treasure she'd thought she'd lost.

He planted a swift kiss on her temple.

"By the way," he said. "I'll be sleeping here from tomorrow night on. Just in case you get some ideas in the middle of the night that can't wait."

She already had one, and she was pretty sure he knew what it was.

Dear Reader,

What a thrill it is to write this first reader letter. I am so grateful to my agent, Kevan Lyon, and my editor, Charles Griemsman, for making this happen. I have always wanted to write a book about high school teachers and coaches, and now this dream is a reality. I was once a high school English teacher like Rosalie, the heroine of this book. Perhaps my involvement with teens and sports explains why I've always had a bit of a love affair with football coaches. There is something about the caged energy they display on the sidelines—a tense expectation that can translate in a second to fist-pumping jubilation. How rewarding it must be to guide young men into adulthood.

This book also explores my first attempt at writing a teenager as the secret baby my heroine raised. I hope you enjoy Danny. It's easy to love a cute little baby, but a teenager with all that angst and willfulness—if you've had one, you know.

Welcome to Whistler Creek, Georgia. Enjoy your stay.

Cynthia

I love to hear from readers. Please send me your reaction to *His Most Important Win* at Cynthoma@aol.com. Or visit my website cynthiathomason.com and watch for my blogs at harlequin.com

His Most Important Win

CYNTHIA THOMASON

MILLS & BOON®

All the characters in this book have no existence outside
the imagination of the author, and have no relation
whatsoever to anyone bearing the same name or names.
They are not even distantly inspired by any individual
known or unknown to the author, and all the incidents
are pure invention.

All Rights Reserved including the right of reproduction
in whole or in part in any form. This edition is published
by arrangement with Harlequin Enterprises II BV/S.à.r.l.
The text of this publication or any part thereof may
not be reproduced or transmitted in any form or
by any means, electronic or mechanical, including
photocopying, recording, storage in an information
retrieval system, or otherwise, without the written
permission of the publisher.

® and TM are trademarks owned and used by the
trademark owner and/or its licensee. Trademarks marked
with ® are registered with the United Kingdom Patent
Office and/or the Office for Harmonisation in the
Internal Market and in other countries.

First published in Great Britain 2012
by Mills & Boon, an imprint of Harlequin (UK) Limited.
Large Print edition 2012
Harlequin (UK) Limited,
Eton House, 18-24 Paradise Road,
Richmond, Surrey TW9 1SR

© Cynthia Thomason 2012

ISBN: 978 0 263 23020 8

Harlequin (UK) policy is to use papers that are natural,
renewable and recyclable products and made from
wood grown in sustainable forests. The logging
and manufacturing process conform to the legal
environmental regulations of the country of origin.

Printed and bound in Great Britain
by CPI Antony Rowe, Chippenham, Wiltshire

CYNTHIA THOMASON

writes contemporary and historical romances and dabbles in mysteries. She has won a National Readers' Choice Award and the 2008 Golden Quill. When she's not writing, she works as a licensed auctioneer for the auction company she and her husband own. As an estate buyer for the auction, she has come across unusual items, many of which have found their way into her books. She has one son, an entertainment reporter. Cynthia dreams of perching on a mountaintop in North Carolina every autumn to watch the leaves turn. You can read more about her at www.cynthiathomason.com

20227509

MORAY COUNCIL
LIBRARIES &
INFORMATION SERVICES

This book is dedicated to the memory of my loving parents, Barbara and Bert Brackett, who never missed a high school football game under the "Friday night lights" of Cuyahoga Falls, Ohio.

Chapter One

Rosalie pulled into one of the last remaining spots in the parking lot, got out of her car and checked her watch. "Three minutes," she grumbled. "I'll just make it if I run." She still had no idea why the high school principal had called this emergency meeting. His secretary had said he wanted as many of his faculty members who were in town to attend, so Rosalie had missed a lasagna dinner with her mother and her son to be here.

"Hey, Rosalie, wait up."

Spotting her friend and fellow teacher

coming across the pavement, Rosalie motioned for Shelby to hustle. "At least there's someone who's even later than I am," she said when Shelby had fallen into step beside her. "Do you know what this is about?"

"No clue," Shelby said. "But I'd rather be anywhere but here. The last thing I want to think about in July is school."

Rosalie held the door open to the three-story brick building and let Shelby go in ahead of her. "I hope Canfield's not expecting us to volunteer for landscaping duty this summer," she said. "I'm working more hours at Mom's produce stand, and I've increased my hours at the Brighter Day Center."

"Why's that? Have there been any deaths in town recently that I haven't heard about?"

"No, but grief is an ongoing thing. The more we volunteers can counsel grieving kids at the center, the faster they can get on with their lives."

Shelby frowned. "I wonder if being around all that sadness is really good for you, Rosalie."

"It's been sixteen years since my brother died, Shel."

"Okay, message received. Forget I said anything."

They approached the media center at the end of the school's main hallway. The doors were open. Rosalie caught the subtle aroma of old books, always a welcoming scent to English teachers or anyone who spent a good part of their childhood nestled in a corner of a library. Once they entered the room, the delicious mustiness would be combined with the even subtler smell of modern-day plastic coming from the bank of computers taking up an entire wall.

The media center was buzzing with activity. Apparently Principal Canfield's calling tree system had worked. Rosalie estimated that nearly three-quarters of the faculty were present along with dozens of booster parents and prominent citizens.

Dexter Canfield, dressed in tan pants and a golf shirt, stood behind the media director's desk chatting with a group of Whistler Creek's most influential citizens including Roland Benton, owner of the town's largest employer, Benton Farms. When Canfield pounded a gavel, the hundred or so attendees stared up at him. Rosalie and Shelby spoke quick greetings to fellow faculty members and took seats in the back.

In his most impressive baritone, the voice Canfield reserved for public address announcements and greetings at halftime sporting events, he thanked everyone for coming and assured the crowd they would not be disappointed. Wasting no time, he proclaimed that a stroke of unbelievable good fortune had befallen the town of Whistler Creek.

"We all regret the recent retirement of Bucky Lowell," he said. Heads nodded. The revered football coach had been an institution at Whistler Creek High for as long as Rosalie could remember. At the end of the last school year, on the advice of his doctor, the seventy-three-year-old Bucky had stowed away his whistle and closed his game book for the last time. Since then speculations had run wild about who the board would hire to replace him. The man had never had a losing season, a record no other Georgia high school coach had achieved.

"Well, hang on to your hats, ladies and gentlemen," Canfield said, "because Bucky's replacement is waiting to come into the room. He signed a contract yesterday, and I think you'll all agree that the Wildcats couldn't have made a better pick if we'd ordered his credentials from the Almighty."

Rosalie studied the expressions of those around her. Some faculty members chuckled. Others shook their heads in bewilderment. A few mumbled guesses about who could possibly fill the shoes of the great Bucky. And then the wait was over. Canfield went to the door of a storage room, opened it wide and in stepped one of Whistler Creek's native sons and former honored gridiron star. He was also the heir to Benton Farms, the area's largest agribusiness and supplier of produce to much of the U.S. Southeast.

When recognition dawned among the old-timers, enthusiastic applause broke out. And Rosalie couldn't seem to draw a breath. It couldn't be. It was. Bryce Benton, wearing a Texas Tech Athletic T-shirt and ball cap, strode to the desk and stood with his hands clasped in front of him waiting for Dexter Canfield to say something.

Rosalie hadn't spoken to Bryce in over fifteen years. She'd only spotted him in town a couple times since he'd left for college, and she'd always turned the other way. But looking at him now, exuding a casual confidence that came with pedigree, adulation and just the right amount of sun-weathered texture to his skin, she felt the years melt away. She swallowed. For all her efforts to move on with her life, she could have been seventeen again.

She'd never dreamed Bryce would give up his career at Texas Tech. But here he was. For some inexplicable reason, he'd apparently chosen to abandon his upward climb at the university to come home and coach at little old Whistler Creek High. Bryce was the onetime all-state wide receiver of the Whistler Creek Wildcats, the future agribusiness magnate and, most important, devastating to Rosalie on so many levels, he was her son Danny's biological father.

Shelby snickered. "What the hell is Canfield doing? Looks like he's bringing his prize stallion into the show ring for all to admire." She nudged Rosalie in her ribs. "And he definitely is a prize!"

Somehow Rosalie found her voice. "You don't know Bryce, do you?"

Shelby, who'd come to Whistler Creek only three years before, grinned. "Not yet. Is he single?"

"Divorced." Whistler Creek was a small town, and over the years the most important details of Bryce's life had filtered down to Rosalie. Not that she'd asked to hear them.

She stared at the tabletop in front of her. She

couldn't look at him, couldn't stand to watch that ruggedly handsome face turn smug with the praise of a public that had obviously forgotten all the details of Bryce's background. Forgotten or forgiven.

Thinking back to when she was a gullible teenager, she felt a flush of shame heat her cheeks. She had once believed she was in love with Bryce Benton, the very same guy who'd just allowed himself to be paraded into the limelight of his expectant hometown crowd as if he were Dexter Canfield's gift to the people of Whistler Creek.

Some mistakes could never be lived down. And some just hurt forever.

Standing in front of people he'd never met before as well as old friends he hadn't seen in years, Bryce felt like a damn fool. Canfield had told him to wait in the wings until he'd made the announcement just so he could pique the interest of the crowd. Bryce had argued that such a plan was ridiculous, but in the end, he'd let Canfield have his way thinking maybe it was better that Dexter prepared the crowd for the return of a prodigal son. Bryce had only come home to Whistler Creek a couple dozen times in the last fifteen years. Now, with something like one hundred pairs of eyes drilling into him, he knew he'd been manipulated into being the featured sideshow event for Canfield's three-ring circus.

He shook his head, raised his hands palms up in an effort to stop the flow of excited chatter that filled the room. When he'd been offered the job to replace Bucky, he'd jumped at the chance. Coaching at Whistler Creek was what he wanted. His goal since college had always been to mentor and guide high school kids on the verge of manhood and possible greatness. Despite the tragedy that would always haunt him, coming home to the town and school that had nurtured him through the years had been the fulfillment of a dream. Now he felt like a trick pony waiting to be led through his paces.

Beaming at Bryce, Canfield said, "I coaxed

him away from Texas Tech, and I wanted all of you to share in this victory for the Whistler Creek High Athletic Department."

Coaxed him away, Bryce thought. He'd taken a ten thousand a year pay cut to be here, and still signed on the bottom line without a moment's hesitation. Most people would say he should have his head examined.

But Bryce gambled on possibilities. And the options for changing lives at the head coaching level at Whistler Creek far surpassed those as the assistant offensive coach at Texas Tech. And then there was his dad, who was sitting here tonight. His health had suffered a blow. He needed his son, wanted him to come home.

He looked into his dad's eyes now, saw the pride there and took a deep breath. "Folks, you all have a seat. This isn't so much a celebration as a chance to get acquainted. Or *reacquainted* as is the case with many of you."

"Are you kidding, Bryce," the president of the Georgia State Bank shouted from the side of the room. "This could be the best football season we've ever had."

Bryce tried to smile and slanted a glance at Bucky Lowell who sat nearby. "I don't know about that," Bryce said, gesturing at Bucky. "Coach Lowell here has left me some pretty big shoes to fill, so let's not get ahead of ourselves. We've all got a lot of work to do. The players, the coaching staff, most of all, me. I think we should save the celebrating until we get a few wins under our belts."

Dexter Canfield continued to grin like the top salesman on a used car lot. "Now you see why I called you here today. We appreciate everything Bucky has done for this program, but today is the beginning of a new era for Whistler Creek athletics. We need to start now, preparing our boys, getting behind our new coach, redoubling our efforts as Wildcat parents and supporters."

"I appreciate all the enthusiasm tonight and in the future," Bryce said. "But let's remember that the ones who need our support most are the young men who'll soon sweat their guts out on the field once practice starts." He paused before adding, "Football in Whistler Creek always has been, and will continue to be, a community effort. Thanks for coming today and for giving me this welcome. But as far as I'm concerned, you can all go on home now, knowing that my office in the athletic building is always open."

He remembered the furor surrounding games in the past and doubted Bucky had kept that same open-door policy for his many years at Whistler. Bryce hoped he wouldn't regret making that statement.

As the meeting wound down, he endured countless handshakes and pats on the back before the last of his well-wishers left the media center. Then he said goodbye to Canfield and walked with his father to the school parking lot. When they stepped into the humid July air of a South Georgia evening, Bryce took his dad's elbow and held him back. "Let's wait until everyone is in their cars," he said.

Roland Benton smiled. "A little uncomfortable with all this excitement, are you, son?"

"Yeah. I didn't anticipate this kind of welcome. I've been gone a long time."

"True, but you've always wanted to come back."

Bryce waved to a man who put down his car window and gave him a thumbs-up sign. "I didn't think it would be like this. You know how it is, Dad. When expectations run too high, everyone can end up disappointed and disillusioned."

"Just do your job, Bryce," Roland said. "No one can ask more. And no one should expect more than your best effort." He smiled. "That's all you'll ask of the players, right?"

"True enough." Seeing the parking lot emptying out, Bryce stepped onto the pavement. He saw two women chatting between cars about a hundred feet down the lot. He stared for a moment before a familiar pang pierced his heart. Could it be? He recognized the lush curls of black hair that fell to one woman's shoulders. "Dad, isn't that Rosalie Campano?"

Roland squinted. "Sure is."

"Is her mother still running her produce stand on Fox Hollow Road?"

"Yes, indeed. Claudia is one of our best local customers. Rosalie still lives with her. You know Rosalie teaches at the high school now?"

"Yeah. Mom told me that a few years back. I should have known she'd be here when I heard Canfield had called the faculty out for this show." Bryce had thought a lot about Rosalie over the years. She'd been an important part of his life at one time—until the day he'd brought so much grief into hers.

Rosalie laughed as she carried on a conversation with the other woman. Bryce recalled the bright, bubbly sound of her voice. "Is her name still Campano?" he asked.

"You mean did she ever get married?"

"Yeah."

"No. She's single. Came close a time or two from what I understand, but it didn't work out."

Rosalie had never married? Bryce tried to rein in his careening thoughts. Roland took Bryce's arm and gently tugged him toward their car parked in the opposite direction.

"Wait," Bryce said, knowing he could be treading on emotional quicksand. "I want to say hello."

"Maybe now's not a good time…"

"Why not? I'm going to be seeing a lot of Rosalie. We'll be working in the same building, maybe teaching some of the same kids." Bryce was already several steps ahead of his dad. "Now's the perfect time."

It was crazy. Bryce knew that. But the closer he got to Rosalie, the more his heart pounded. For Pete's sake. It had been almost sixteen years since Ricky had died. They'd each gone on with their lives. But heck, she was right there across the lot, where she couldn't refuse his phone calls. Bryce always wondered if maybe he'd get the chance to tell her again how sorry he was for what happened. So he quickened his footsteps.

And then she looked up and trapped his gaze. It was only a quick glance, almost as if she hadn't noticed him at all. But her smile faded and she turned again to her friend, said something brief and got in her car. Bryce stopped dead. Before he could have reached her, she'd backed her red compact car out of its space and was headed to the street.

And for the second time that night, Bryce felt like an idiot.

Chapter Two

Shortly after the meeting at the high school broke up, Rosalie came in the back door of the home she still lived in with her mother. She reached down and scratched behind Dixie's ear. The golden retriever nuzzled her soft nose against Rosalie's jeans. The scent of fresh baked bread and pungent Italian spices filled the welcoming kitchen. A half-filled dish of lasagna sat on the table along with the remains of a salad in a seasoned wooden bowl. Rosalie called out, "Mom, you here?"

Drying her hands on a towel, Claudia came

out of the pantry. "There's plenty of lasagna left, Rosalie," she said. "I'll heat up a plateful if you're hungry."

"No, thanks. I'm going out in a little while."

"Oh? You seeing Ted?"

Her mother was one of the few people who knew Rosalie had accepted a few dates with Whistler Creek High's baseball coach. Rosalie tried to keep her personal life private. "No. He's got his kids this weekend. I'm meeting Shelby downtown at the Creek Side Tavern." She stepped to the entry to the living room and looked around. "Is Danny here?"

"No. His friends picked him up twenty minutes ago."

Rosalie sighed with relief, pulled out a kitchen chair and slumped into it. "Good. I don't have to pretend that everything's okay then."

"You certainly don't have to pretend with me," Claudia said. "I've already heard. Sharon Potter was at the meeting and she called me when she got home."

"Then you know about our new football coach."

"I know." Claudia shook her head. "I always thought Bryce would come back here, especially after his divorce. And now his father had that bypass surgery…"

Rosalie blew out a long breath. "I always prayed he wouldn't return."

Claudia pulled out a chair and sat across the table from her daughter. "Don't borrow trouble, Rosalie. Just because Bryce is back doesn't mean that anything has to change."

Rosalie sighed deeply. "I think *everything* will change, for me at least. I'll have to face him at school every day this fall and I might even run into him at Benton Farms when I go there to pick up your produce orders."

Then a startling realization occurred to her and she stared at her mother. "Like tomorrow," she said. "I promised you I'd go to Benton's in the morning. What if Bryce is there?"

Claudia squeezed her hand. "I don't know where Bryce is staying, but even if he is out at his parents' place, you can go to the market early, before most normal people are even out of bed."

Rosalie nodded. "Yeah, I can do that. But Mom, having Bryce return to Whistler Creek feels a little like adding gasoline to a long-simmering fire." She raised her hands. "Ka-boom."

"You're jumping to conclusions, Rosalie. The secret has remained buried since Danny was born. That's a long time. Only four people are alive in this town who even know that Bryce is Danny's father. None of us has ever broken the promise we made that night." She frowned and looked away.

Rosalie recalled that stressful meeting at the Benton home nearly sixteen years ago. Claudia Campano had briefly argued in favor of letting Bryce know about Rosalie's pregnancy, but she had quickly capitulated to everyone else's desires.

Rosalie picked up a slice of bread from a basket at the center of the table and began shredding it. "I wish I were as confident as you, Mom. But in the back of my mind I picture Bryce coming face-to-face with Danny, and just, well, *knowing.* Like this cosmic bond will connect the two of them."

Claudia took the mutilated bread from Rosalie's hand. "That's not going to happen, honey. We've always been careful. Growing up, Danny never questioned your story about his father."

"That's because Poppa was still alive and he was the only father Danny ever needed. He was better to Danny than anyone else could have been." Rosalie clasped her hands on top of the table. "I never told you, Mom, but last year, a few months after Poppa died, Danny asked me about his real father."

"And what did you tell him?"

"I kept up the pretense I'd established before—that his father and I only knew each other a short time." *That was a lie.* She'd known Bryce all her life. "That we were only together one time." *That was the truth.* "That his father was not ready to assume the responsibility of a baby." *That was the truth.* "And I told Danny again that I loved him from the moment I knew he existed, and you and Poppa loved him as if he were your own, too."

Claudia nodded. "And was Danny satisfied?"

"I guess. I appeased him by promising that later, if he wanted to try and find his father, I would help him do that. Of course, I hoped that he would never ask."

"And he hasn't," Claudia said. "Just because Bryce is back in town doesn't have to mean anything. The physical resemblance is almost nonexistent. Danny need never know." Her eyes widened as her lips turned up in a strange sort of smile. "Unless you decide to tell him."

"What? Mom, I can't see that as a possibility." Rosalie pressed her finger against the bridge of her nose where a headache was just beginning to form. "I wish I didn't have this feeling of foreboding, like something terrible is going to happen."

"Give this some time, Rosalie. Bryce will settle in. You'll continue with your life—your teaching and your volunteer duties. I've always believed that things just work out for the best— eventually." She touched Rosalie's cheek. "Now, go. Get ready to meet your friends. You need to get your mind on something else."

Rosalie stood, pushed her chair under the table. "I don't think I'm going to be good company." She headed toward the living room but turned around when her mother said her name. "Something else, Mom?"

"Did you talk to him, honey?"

"No. After the meeting he came toward me in the parking lot. I panicked, got in my car and drove away." She bit her bottom lip. She'd never admit that certain instincts, long suppressed, had almost caused her to wait for him to reach her. "I wasn't ready to face him," she said. "I don't think I ever will be."

Claudia nodded. "Time will tell."

"What's that supposed to mean? It's been more than fifteen years. And tonight I learned that all time has told me is that I still react to Bryce Benton."

Trying to put Bryce out of her mind, she went down the hallway toward her room, the cozy, familiar, rosy space that had been her private sanctum all her life. On the way, she stopped at another door, put her hand on the knob and took a deep breath. Her brother's old room, which was now Danny's. For three months after Ricky had died, Rosalie hadn't been able to even look inside this space. Her father, in his attempt to heal his family, had eventually gone in and packed up many of the items Ricky had treasured. He hadn't asked the women of his family to help.

But there had been practical matters to consider. A family had to move on. A baby was coming. They'd ordered a crib and other essentials. This room was needed for the future of the Campano family.

Rosalie turned the knob and opened the door. Although other mementos of Ricky existed in the house—in her mother's room and the living room—the only reminder of Ricky in this space now was a photo of him in his Wildcat uniform. Danny had insisted on keeping the photo of his "Uncle Ricardo," whom he'd never met, on that hutch above his desk.

Rosalie walked into the room and picked up the photo, which was both comfortingly familiar and achingly sad. She smiled at the image of her "second half," the other part of her. With his football helmet tucked against his side, his shoulders unnaturally wide and strong under the padding, his dark hair military short as if he'd prepared for the battle on the football field, Ricky was the picture of invincible confidence.

She touched the tip of her finger to the letters of his jersey. She'd been so proud of him, the Wildcats star quarterback, recipient of a scholarship to Florida State University. Even now, looking at his cocky smile, her heart melted.

"I miss you," she said to the quiet room. She still felt his presence in every square foot of the Campano house, but especially here. Could anything really separate twins? Not time. Not even death.

Setting the photo back on the shelf, she looked

around at the things that identified her Danny. A baseball bat signed by Alex Rodriquez. A weathered mitt he'd outgrown after three seasons of Little League. Pictures of his heroes on the walls—current Atlanta Braves, legendary New York Yankees. A photo of Danny in his junior varsity baseball uniform. Soon that would be replaced by his freshman picture in a varsity uniform when he would take the mound as the Wildcats newest star pitcher.

By Danny's third birthday, Rosalie had known he would be an athlete. He'd had the passion, the determination and the skinned knees to prove it. When, at a very young age, he had picked up a football he'd found in the park, her heart had seemed to stop beating for several long, painful seconds until she'd taken it from his hands. That very day she brought him to the sporting goods store and introduced him to every other sport. He'd settled on baseball and she'd encouraged him through all his years.

She'd never been sorry she'd pushed him in

that direction. Once, when he had mentioned trying out for the football team, she had discouraged him, saying his talents lay on the diamond, not the gridiron. He'd accepted her advice, and he'd thrived. He'd proven himself. Most important, she'd been able to watch his progress from the bleachers without fearing that the next moment, the next play, could alter his life forever. She couldn't go through that again. Much like she couldn't face Bryce Benton.

She closed the door to Danny's room and went to shower and dress. She'd make it an early night so she could do as her mother suggested and be at Benton Farms first thing the next morning. While Bryce and most of the world slept in, she'd pick up her order and be gone.

Benton Farms was located five miles outside of Whistler Creek on a two-lane road that wound through rolling hills, green pastures and what real estate agents called some of the best farmland in America. At 6:50 a.m., after pulling on jeans and an old T-shirt and fastening her unruly hair in a clip, Rosalie sipped coffee from a thermal mug as she chugged along the sparsely populated route in the old pickup Claudia had purchased for her produce business.

Over the years Rosalie had managed to maintain a working relationship with the Bentons despite the heartache their son had brought into her life. And she'd been grateful Danny had inherited the dark eyes and olive complexion of the Campanos and not the lighter skin tones and fair hair of the Bentons. No one in town had ever suspected that the onetime childhood friends, Rosie and Bryce, had ever conceived a child. And Rosalie had further protected her son's identity by slightly modifying his birth records.

Today she planned to be first in line to drive through the wholesale distribution section of Benton's corporate sales area which opened to local buyers at 7:00 a.m. Rising before dawn hadn't been a problem. After coming home from dinner with friends, Rosalie had slept restlessly. Finally she'd kept one eyelid raised to her window, watching for the first hint of a pink sunrise on the eastern horizon.

Her mind raced with the possible ramifications of last evening's odd turn of events. Why had Bryce sacrificed his climb up the university coaching ladder? Did he miss his hometown that much? Did he feel an obligation to his parents? Had the divorce she'd heard about set him back emotionally so that his return to Whistler Creek was as much a healing exercise as anything else? Rosalie could almost understand that explanation. She couldn't imagine living anywhere else herself.

But Bryce, at least the young man she'd known and fancied herself in love with, had always displayed enough confidence to combat any of life's trials. Surely he could handle news of his father's declining health, the breakup of a marriage. After all, he'd recovered easily enough from the death of his best friend.

And why had he approached her in the parking lot yesterday? Did he suspect the truth about her quick getaway—that she'd seen him and was avoiding a face-to-face meeting? She'd tried to appear casual, spontaneous, as if she hadn't noticed him. She hoped he'd believed that a sudden thought had occurred to her and she'd naturally and without ulterior motive gotten into her car and sped away. And if not, did he suspect the other, more devastating truth, that facing him, dredging up memories, both good and bad, possibly initiating new ones, was the last thing she needed in her life?

Thankful that the electric gates had been parted a few minutes early, Rosalie drove onto Benton property and headed a quarter mile down the road toward the steel buildings that housed the wholesale division of Benton Farms. As she pulled up next to the overstuffed bins of vegetables, she noticed that she was the first local produce dealer to arrive. The usual farmhands, wearing the trademark green Benton Farms polo shirts, waved at her as they always did. She knew each of them would be willing to help her choose her stock and load it into the back of the truck.

She climbed out of the driver's seat and spoke to Juan Gonzalez. He'd been hired by Roland Benton to work under her father's direction when Enzo Campano had supervised the wholesale area. Rosalie had known him since she was a little girl.

"Juan, I need red peppers today and ten bushels of corn. Maybe eight pounds of Vidalia onions." She handed him her list.

"I get you set up in no time, Miss Rosalie." He began loading cartons while she walked among the bins of rich, ripe crops recently harvested on Benton land.

She picked up a tomato and was deciding if this particular one was overripe when a hand settled lightly on her shoulder and a familiar voice spoke into her ear. "Hello, Rosalie. Been a long time."

She jerked as if his fingers had delivered an electric shock to her nervous system, whirled around and dropped the tomato on the pavement. It exploded into a pulpy mass, which immediately attracted a number of tiny winged insects. Rosalie swallowed and looked up into clear blue eyes that had haunted her teenaged dreams. She swore under her breath. What the hell was Bryce doing out here at the crack of dawn? Her voice came out dry and tinny sounding when she frowned down at the mess by her sneaker. "Sorry about that," she said.

Dressed in the same Benton Farms shirt as the other employees, Bryce grabbed a paper towel from a nearby dispenser and bent over to scoop up the mess. "No problem." He swept his other hand over the loaded cartons of tomatoes. "As you can see, we have a few others."

He tossed the soggy towel into a trash can and wiped his hand on his jeans. If he'd planned to shake hands with her, he changed his mind. Thank goodness. Rosalie didn't need to test her reaction to another touch.

"I saw you last night at the high school," he said.

She blinked a couple times, trying to blur the image of Bryce's face that seemed determined to burn itself into her retina. Last night he'd worn a ball cap low over his forehead, and he'd been at the other side of the room. Today his features were clear, undiluted by shadow and the play of artificial light. And she would have known him anywhere. Just as she remembered, the corner of his mouth quirked up in an odd half grin. His eyes, nearly the rich color of blueberries, narrowed under thick, brown lashes. Strands of his hair, longer than she would have thought he'd like and darker blond than she recalled, fell to the arch of his slightly darker eyebrows.

He continued to pin her with a disturbingly intense gaze as the grin broadened. "Rosalie? You okay?"

Of course he would ask that. She'd been standing for several awkward moments hoping her senses would return along with enough intelligible words so she wouldn't sound like an idiot. She shook her head, trying to clear her mind. What had he said? Something about seeing her at the high school. Hunching one shoulder with feigned indifference, she said, "I was there. Canfield wanted all the faculty to witness…"

She stopped, knowing she was about to finish the sentence with a biting example of sarcasm.

"…the spectacle?" Bryce filled in for her.

"I wasn't going to say that." Sure she wasn't. That was the exact word that had popped into her mind.

He chuckled. "Well, that's what it was. Only an appearance by the Wildcat marching band could have been worse."

"Obviously your return is viewed as a miracle by some people around here. Who better to take over for Bucky than a hometown football hero?" A shudder rippled down Rosalie's spine. She really hadn't meant to sound so unkind. A better plan would be to appear totally indifferent to Bryce.

"I guess we'll see about that," he said.

"Miss Rosalie!" The call came from a few yards away.

She stood on tiptoe to see over Bryce's shoulder. "That's Juan by my truck. He must have my order together."

"I'll give him a hand."

Bryce stood aside as she walked ahead of him to the pickup where her order was stacked on the pavement. Knowing he was behind her made the skin at the nape of her neck prickle. Her footsteps felt leaden; the distance of only a few yards to her truck was like the length of a football field.

A line of trucks and trailers had started to form behind her. "We'd better hurry and get this loaded," she said. "You have other customers."

The three of them filled the pickup's cargo area. Rosalie quickly consulted her list and wrote a check. When she tore it out of the book, she hesitated, looking first at Juan and then Bryce. "Who do I give this to?"

"Give it to Juan," Bryce said. "He's the boss. I'm just here to do what I can."

She handed over the check and opened the door to the truck. "I suppose your father is happy you're back."

"He seems to be. I hope I can be more of a help than a hindrance."

She climbed inside the truck, shut the door and started the engine. Bryce leaned on her open window. "Funny, but as soon as I got out here among the harvest this morning, it all came back to me," he said. "I suppose produce is in my blood."

"And football," she said.

"Yep. And football."

Rosalie stared out her windshield. All she had to do was put the truck in gear, and this whole anxiety-inducing episode would be over. She'd survived a face-to-face with Bryce. Maybe she could even walk by him in the halls of Whistler Creek High School without dissolving into a mass of insecurities. Not risking another look at his face, she lifted her hand. "Well, see you. Say hi to your parents."

"I will. Give my regards to Claudia."

"Sure thing." Eyes straight ahead. Lips tight. Truck shifted into drive.

Now just take your foot off the brake....

"Oh, Rosalie," he said, his arm still on her door.

She swiveled her head slightly, just enough to see him out of the corner of her eye. "Yes?"

"You want to get together?"

Now her eyes snapped to his. Was he kidding? No. He actually appeared sincere. "Ah..."

"I'm only working until noon today, just until the out-of-town orders are loaded on trucks. Maybe we could meet at the Whistler Inn for lunch."

"Lunch?" She gripped the steering wheel and resisted the urge to slap her forehead. She was an English teacher for heaven's sake, and all she could muster was monosyllabic responses.

He chuckled. "Yeah. It's the meal in the middle of the day. Most people eat it."

She glowered at him. "I can't do lunch."

"Are you sure? I thought maybe I could catch up on fifteen years of Whistler Creek gossip."

"Bryce, your parents can fill you in on what's happened around here."

"I suppose they could, if all I wanted to know about was the sixty-something country-club set. But I never cared much about those people when I lived here."

Right. You much preferred the simple earthiness of the Campanos. Well, not any more. "Look, I just can't. I'm working at the stand today." That was a lie. Saturday was Rosalie's errand day. She did chores while Danny helped Claudia at the stand. Now she had to hope Bryce didn't stop by.

"Some other time then?"

She eased off the brake, gratified when the truck slipped away from him. "Maybe. Who knows?" she said.

"Rosalie?"

She gingerly stepped on the pedal, slowing the truck to a crawl. "What?"

"I still miss him, too."

She hit the accelerator and drove off. When she looked in her rearview mirror through burning eyes, she saw Bryce standing there, hands on hips, watching her leave.

Chapter Three

Marjorie Benton slid another pancake on top of the stack she'd already layered on Bryce's plate. "You ready for more bacon?" she asked.

He stared up at her. "Mom, enough. I've only been home a few days, and I've probably gained five pounds."

She scooted the syrup bottle closer to him. "It's Sunday, Brycie. We always have big breakfasts on weekends, remember?"

Bryce sought help from his father who remained hidden behind the newspaper. "So that plate of scrambled eggs and sausage that you brought to me in the wholesale market on Friday morning was a light meal?" he said to her.

Roland Benton covered up a chuckle with a rustle of the sports section.

Marjorie sat at the table next to her son. "It wouldn't hurt you to put on a few pounds," she said. "I know you don't cook for yourself as a bachelor…"

He started to tell her that he was a good cook, even had a recipe box in one of the cartons currently stored in the garage, but figured she'd then tell everyone in town about her son, the kitchen wizard. Probably not the best image for the new football coach to project. Besides he could always tell when his mother was on a roll and knew the futility of trying to stop her.

"…I suspect you haven't eaten properly in years," she continued. "I know that woman you were married to didn't like to cook." She paused. "Or keep a clean house."

Bryce smiled around a bite of doughy pancake. It wasn't as if he and *that woman* had lived in squalor for four years. True, Audrey hadn't been the domestic type, but she'd made sure the cleaning lady showed up weekly, so he'd never been able to write his initials in the dust. And she'd mapped out the best take-out restaurants in Lubbock, so when he didn't feel like cooking for the two of them, they'd never gone hungry. Housekeeping issues hadn't been what broke them up.

Marjorie raised one finger in the air. "But…"

Bryce swallowed and washed down the pancake with a big gulp of milk. *Here it comes.*

"I think we should discuss what's really concerning me this morning," his mother said. Behind his newspaper, Roland took a long swallow of coffee.

Bryce set down his fork and pushed away his plate. "Mom, do we really need to go over this?"

She tapped a manicured fingernail on the tabletop. "I don't see why you're meeting with a real estate agent today, Bryce. Give me one good reason why you're rushing into this."

He set his elbows on the table and looked at her. "Mom, would you like to see my driver's license? It's proof that I'm thirty-three years old."

Her spine stiffened. "I know how old you are, Bryce. I was there the day you were born."

"But you haven't been there every day for the last fifteen years," he said. "I'm used to living on my own. I need my own place."

"What's wrong with your old room?"

"Nothing. It has four sturdy walls, a big window overlooking the back patio, a view of the cornfield and the peach orchards. It's a paradise." He took a deep breath. "In fact, I think you and Dad should strip it bare, paint the walls a bright sunny color, move in your sewing machine and cutting table and make it your home hobby center."

"Really, Bryce! I'm only thinking of you."

He glanced at the ceiling as if inspiration, and patience, could be found there before covering her hand with his and once again wishing he weren't an only child. "Mom, I love you. You know that."

She brushed a strand of blond hair off her forehead and sniffed.

"I want a home—my home—and I want it in this town."

She pursed her lips a moment. "*This* is your home, Bryce. What need do your father and I have for this big house?"

"That's a good question," he said. "And one for you and Dad to think about. But for now, I'm tired of living in places that, for the last fifteen years, have always seemed like temporary shelters to me. Dorm rooms, apartments, condos. I want a house, a little bit of land, some grass with honest-to-goodness roots that I can fertilize and watch grow. I've waited a long time for this opportunity to come my way, and I want those roots in Whistler Creek soil. Soil with my name on the deed."

Marjorie looked out the sliding glass doors which opened onto a view of acres and acres of rich Benton farmland. "But all this will eventually *be* your soil, Bryce."

"Maybe so, Mom, and I look forward to helping Dad when he needs me. But for now…"

Marjorie started to speak, but stopped when Roland suddenly made a show of folding the newspaper and setting it on the table. Roland didn't say much, but when he did, everyone in the room generally gave him the floor. "He's a grown man, Marjorie. He's going to contribute to this community in more ways than just as the heir to Benton Farms." Roland leaned forward, leveling a steely gray gaze on his wife's face. "Let him go. What's a few miles between you and him anyway?"

Marjorie fingered the flowery buttons on her robe before standing to her full, impressive five feet eight inches. She picked up Bryce's plate and walked to the sink. "Fine," she snapped, turning the water on full blast.

Bryce sat in the uncomfortable silence for a full minute wondering if he should say something to bridge a gap between his parents which all at once seemed cavernous. And then his father reached across the table for a slice of crisp bacon on a platter. He picked it up and had it halfway to his mouth when Marjorie, the always effective eyes in the back of her head in full operational mode, stormed the table and smacked his hand. "Don't even think about it," she said, pointing to his chest as if his heart had ears.

Roland dropped the bacon, gave his son a little smile and picked up his newspaper.

Bryce stood in the middle of a stand of live oak trees and looked at the front of the weathered clapboard house he'd just toured. Turning to the real estate agent he'd hired, he said, "I can't believe how many times I've driven this road, Lisa, seen this driveway, but never really knew what was back here behind all these trees."

"I'm not surprised," the agent said. "You can't see the structure from the road." She consulted notes in her portfolio. "The house was built in

1953 by a Canadian man, Clive Harbin. It's only had two owners, Clive and his son, who inherited the place and used it as a winter residence since sometime in the '80s. The son, whose name is Wyatt, has been unable to make the trip for the last three years, and the house has remained unoccupied all that time. I guess that's why Wyatt's kids convinced him to sell."

Bryce noted the missing shingles, crumbling bricks on the chimney. "It needs work," he said. "Gutters need to be replaced. The whole house needs painting, inside and out." Even as he listed the home's problems, his hands itched to get to work on it. An hour ago, when he'd cleared the narrow, rutted drive and had his first view of the house, he'd fallen in love with its clean, traditional lines. Now he was trying to keep his enthusiasm at a reasonable level so he wouldn't make a mistake with an offer.

A classic cottage farmhouse, the Realtor had called it. Steep second-story roof, a pair of gabled windows, an inviting porch that extended along the front and wrapped around one side. The inside floor plan met his needs exactly. A big living room with a stone fireplace, nice-size dining room, a kitchen that needed updating but was plenty big enough for a small table and chairs. A master bedroom downstairs with a small bonus room he could use as an office, and two small bedrooms upstairs.

"Let's walk around back," the agent suggested. "It says on my specs that the property extends three hundred yards into the wooded area."

As they made their way around the side of the house, Bryce noted the well and water softener, and a patch of green grass that probably indicated the septic system. The rest of the yard was mostly weeds and overgrown shrubs. "How much total acreage?" he asked when they looked beyond the border of the backyard to a forest of pine, oak and magnolia trees.

"Four-and-a-half acres," Lisa said, looking down at her shoes. "I'm not going into the woods with you in these new heels, but you go ahead."

Bryce walked into the thick forest and returned after a few minutes. His mind buzzed with plans. He'd need to hire a backhoe operator to clear the wild shrubs and scrub trees, buy a decent chainsaw and weed eater....

"So what do you think?" she asked. "When you gave me your wish list, I immediately thought of this place."

"It's the best of the three we've seen," he said.

"And its location on Fox Hollow Road makes it easily accessible to town."

And the Campano's house, Bryce thought. As he was following the agent to this property, he'd passed the home where he'd spent so many happy days growing up. When he'd glanced at the house, his heart had lurched in his chest. For most of his formative years, Bryce had felt as comfortable in the Campano home as he had in his own house. Maybe even more so. He and Ricky and Rosalie had been like siblings, Enzo and Claudia, like second parents.

He'd noticed too, the cars parked at Claudia Campano's roadside stand. Not surprising that on a beautiful Sunday afternoon folks would be stopping for fresh produce. He hadn't seen Rosalie. Bryce made up his mind to stop at the stand on his way back down Fox Hollow Road and say hello to Mrs. Campano.

"What do you want to do?" the agent said, breaking into his thoughts. "I'd love to draw up a contract on this house." She gave him a brilliant smile. "I think it would be perfect for our town's new football coach."

"I'll need to arrange inspections first," he said. "Check for termites. Check the roof, plumbing and electrical."

"Of course. But we can make the contract contingent on the inspections coming in satisfactorily." She tapped a pen on the top of her portfolio. "You don't want to lose this place by not having your name on the dotted line."

He smiled. "How many offers have you had on this property since it was listed last year?" he said.

She shrugged. "Admittedly it's been a slow market."

Bryce was going to own this house. He felt it in the jangle of excited nerves in the pit of his stomach. "It's listed at ninety thousand?"

"That's right."

"Write up an offer at twenty percent under that price. We'll see what happens."

She held out her hand. "Meet me in my office in a half hour. I'll get the paperwork started."

Rosalie joined her son and her mother at the produce stand midafternoon on Sunday. "When are your friends picking you up to go to the park?" she asked Danny.

He checked his watch. "They should be here any minute. I need to get my gear. Are you staying to help Grandma?"

"Yes. You go on."

"Thanks." He pointed to an insufficient number of small baskets of tomatoes sitting in a bin. "You need to restock. I was just getting ready to do that."

"Sure. Looks like it's been a good day."

He agreed, said goodbye to Claudia and

jogged away just as a Honda Civic pulled into the drive and followed him toward the house. Rosalie waved to Danny's friend at the wheel. She took a stack of miniature bushel baskets from under the bin and started to fill them with tomatoes from a large crate. Her attention was diverted when a black pickup with sparkling chrome accessories braked in front of the stand. She immediately noticed a front bumper license plate in black and gold that said Texas Tech University, and a moment later, Bryce Benton got out of the driver's seat.

He started to walk to Rosalie but stopped when Claudia hooted so loud a customer spilled a bag of peaches. "Bryce Benton! Oh, my stars. Get over here."

Bryce strode around the back of the stand and gave Claudia a hug. When she finally let him loose, she placed the flat of her hand over her heart and stared up into his face. "You have gotten even better looking, if that's possible."

Rosalie hurried to the front to help the customer retrieve her peaches. As she worked, she couldn't help thinking that her mother's reaction to seeing Bryce was amazing, and not in a good way. For a time, both women, and Rosalie's father as well, had nurtured bad feelings against Bryce every bit as strong as the ones Rosalie still seemed to cling to.

Numb with grief at the sudden, tragic death of their son, Rosalie's parents had sought comfort in the only way they knew how—by blaming the young man whose show-off antics had resulted in the accident which took the life of his best friend. Looking back, Rosalie realized that the anger and bitterness against Bryce, rightly or wrongly, had probably been the glue that had held the Campano family together through the weeks and months of mourning.

And then Danny came along and their lives progressed according to a new purpose and pace. Rosalie continued to cry every night for her brother. Enzo Campano buried his grief so deep that Rosalie often wondered if he allowed himself to think about Ricky at all. And

Claudia threw her efforts and mothering skills into making a home for her grandson.

Unlike her daughter and her husband, at some point, she'd let go of the anguish and resentment. At least she said she had. But had she ever really forgiven Bryce? Since the Campanos didn't talk much about the incident, Rosalie had always wondered. Today, however, almost sixteen years after her son's death, Claudia tried to convince her daughter in this grandiose gesture of welcoming Bryce home that she had.

"You're the talk of the town, Bryce," Claudia said. He grinned in a seemingly modest way and chatted quietly with her.

Rosalie rang up the customer's order. When the lady got in her car and drove away, Bryce walked over. "So how's business, Rosalie?" he said.

"It's okay."

The Honda sped past with Danny in the backseat. The driver honked his horn and turned onto Fox Hollow Road.

Bryce stared at the car for a moment and then snapped his fingers. "That's right. You have a kid, don't you? My mother told me you went to college, met a guy and had a baby."

"That's right."

"A boy?"

"Yes."

"And you moved back home with Claudia?"

"Right again."

The car rounded a curve and disappeared. Rosalie hoped that would be the end of the conversation. Nope.

"Is your son in high school yet?" Bryce asked.

Vague. Vague. Keep your answers vague. Divert attention away from Danny. "Starts this year," she said, returning to the task of packing tomato boxes. Bryce didn't take the hint and move away, so she looked up at him, swallowed an involuntary sigh, and said, "You're surrounded by fruits and vegetables at your house, Bryce, so you're obviously not here to shop."

He smiled. "Not today."

"Then…?"

He leaned a hip against the stand. "Campanos does business with Benton Farms, and I'm grateful for your years of support. Would you believe it's customer appreciation day?"

Right. She rearranged tomatoes to fit more boxes in the bin. "Not unless this magnanimous event just started today."

"As a matter of fact, it did."

She huffed. "And exactly how many Benton customers have you visited so far to show your appreciation?"

The grin broadened. "You're the first."

She frowned at him and continued working, though on some deeper emotional level she was aware of his every move. "As you can see, I'm busy. If you want to go appreciate someone else, feel free."

"I stopped by for another reason, too," he said.

"And that would be?"

He stood straight and looked down the road. "You and I are going to be neighbors."

Her hand stilled. She clutched her fists at her sides. "What are you talking about?"

"I'm about to become a home owner. I put a bid in for a place down the road, about halfway between your house and the old gristmill."

Her mind scrambled to come up with a location. Houses were separated by acres of land on Fox Hollow Road. There were no close neighbors in the traditional sense. The only property she knew of that was for sale was the old Harbin place. Surely he didn't mean the homestead that was less than a mile away.

"I just left the Harbin property," he said. "I've made an offer."

She could only stare, reining in her first impulse to shout at him that he had no right. That she didn't want him living so near. That she didn't need to be thinking about him driving past her house every day, invading the space in her heart that once had been filled with him. Instead, after a few moments she found her voice. "That place has been vacant for quite a while."

"I know. It needs some work. Have you ever driven back there to see the house?"

She had once or twice, when she was a kid. But she couldn't tell him right now what the house even looked like. "My dad knew old Mr. Clive," she said. "And he sometimes drove produce out to Wyatt Harbin when he was in town. I don't remember much about the place. The people who stayed there kept to themselves."

Light animated Bryce's eyes. "It's a great place, Rosalie. Got real potential. I can't wait to start fixing it up."

It wasn't enough that she was going to work with Bryce at the high school. Now they were going to be neighbors. In a spread-out, rural community the size of Whistler Creek, why hadn't he found a house miles away on one of the other country roads?

She realized he was talking and forced herself to tune in.

"...a done deal yet. The family will have to accept the offer...." He stopped, stared at her. "But I really want that house, Rosalie. I'll start to feel more like a part of the community once I've moved in." He waited for a reaction from her and when he didn't get one he said, "Aren't you going to congratulate me?"

At the risk of choking she said, "Congratulations, Bryce." She almost said, *Once again you'll get everything you want,* but instead said the words she knew her eavesdropping mother would be waiting for. "I hope you're happy in the new place."

He smiled. "Since we'll be living so close, maybe you'll bring me a cup of sugar if I need to borrow it."

That was the last straw. In spite of Claudia's listening to every word, Rosalie said, "Look around you, Bryce. Nothing but fields and barns and open space. This isn't Wisteria Lane for heaven's sake. We don't meet in the mornings for coffee and in the afternoons for margaritas."

She spared a glance in her mother's direction and immediately felt the sting of her heated gaze. *Well, sorry, Ma.*

"I'm kind of disappointed to hear that, Rosalie," Bryce said. "I was hoping we could put the past behind us."

Rosalie let out a long breath and with it, some of the anger trapped in her chest. "Bryce, I hope you become the best football coach this town has ever known. And I hope you get as much out of this job as you can. I really do. But as far as you and I are concerned, the past will always be an issue. It won't go away. It shaped us, made us who we are." *And I won't let your coming back to town change the woman I've become now. I can't.*

He crossed his arms over his chest and gave her an intense stare. "Rosalie, Ricky was the best friend I ever had," he said so only she could hear. "You were the second-best until one day you became so much more. I can't forget that. I don't want to forget it."

"Then you'll have to live with it any way you can. That's what I've had to do."

He started to say something but stopped when two cars pulled into the lot. Excited passengers spilled out of the doors and headed to the stand. Bryce gave her one last look, filled with sadness and longing. "I'll see you around, Rosie-girl," he said, calling her by a former pet name. "But it's all just a damn shame."

"That we can agree on," she said.

He said goodbye to Claudia, got in his truck and drove off. And Rosalie began greeting customers. Anything to avoid the censure in her mother's eyes and an old longing that was trying to squeeze its way into her heart.

Chapter Four

Live with it any way you can.

Those words spoken by Rosalie at the Campano produce stand yesterday continued to haunt Bryce as he dressed in shorts and a T-shirt for his first official visit to Whistler Creek High School's athletic building. Without giving his mother a chance to discuss the real estate deal he'd entered into Sunday afternoon, he gave her a peck on her cheek, poured himself a mug of coffee and dashed out the door to his truck. He didn't feel up to another argument this morning.

"What is it exactly that Rosalie expects of me?" he said aloud as he drove down the wide country road bordered by estate homes and green patches of rich, fertile farmland.

Obviously nothing, you thickheaded dolt!

The truck's air-conditioning blasted him over the rim of the mug as he took a swig of steaming coffee. "And why the hell can't you leave it at that?" he added, setting the cup into the drink holder.

Of course, he knew the answer to that question. Once Rosalie had mattered to him more than any other person he'd ever known. She and Ricky had been his constant companions for years. And then, one brilliant spring day at the end of their senior year in high school, he'd realized he was crazy in love with Rosie. Nothing in his life so far had equaled the pure, sweet jubilation, nor packed the emotional wallop, of that moment.

Thinking back now, it seemed to Bryce that Rosalie had come to the same conclusion as he had at the exact same minute in time on the momentous morning one day after their senior prom. Neither of their dates had made it to the ritual breakfast, this year hosted at the Benton home on Little River Road. Rosalie's date, nursing a headache from too much booze the night before, had gone to church at his parents' insistence. Bryce's date, the girl he'd been with since his junior year, had slept in, refusing to even pick up the phone when he'd called that morning to rouse her.

Suddenly finding themselves stag at a date affair, and totally comfortable with each other, Bryce and Rosalie had wandered into the peach orchard with two wineglasses, a pitcher of fresh orange juice and a chilled bottle of champagne Bryce had pilfered from his father's wine cellar. They'd laughed at the pop of the cork and jumped back as the frothing liquid had poured from the bottle, sending sparkles of golden wine over Rosalie's flowered sundress.

Bryce made the mimosas a little strong, handed Rosalie a glass and suggested they wrap their arms in a traditional romantic toast.

All fun and games, right? They'd sipped and smiled at each other as if they were Hollywood romance legends. Rosalie had batted those long black lashes that every girl in high school had envied, and Bryce leaned in to give her a kiss on her cheek. That's what he'd intended. Only the force of some crazy cosmic collision seemed to take control of his body and he'd claimed her lips. To this day he didn't know why. He only knew that when their mouths touched, hers soft as the peach-scented breeze that morning, his greedy and seeking, nothing had ever been the same.

Bryce navigated the moderate traffic of downtown Whistler Creek to the high school and parked in the lot reserved for teachers. Only one other car was there, a gray SUV with a faculty sticker on the windshield. He took cartons from the back of his truck, loaded them onto a two-wheeled cart and walked past the high school. Taking the track around the football field, he came to the freestanding athletic center where his office was located. The building had been dedicated ten years earlier, thanks to public tax dollars, corporate donations and too many bake sales to count.

Dexter Canfield had given Bryce a key to the facility, so he unlocked the door and went inside. The smells of sweat and socks and the indefinable scent of masculine dreams greeted him as he walked down a short hallway decorated with commemorative bricks inscribed with contributor names. Bryce stopped long enough to read the name *Benton Farms* in the short list of $5,000 benefactors. He entered the first office on the right where the name plaque on the door already said "Coach Benton."

The office had been cleaned out in preparation for his takeover. Someone had spackled over reminders of the previous occupant's certificates and photos. Fresh beige paint covered the walls. The large metal desk in the center of the room was free of clutter, and Bryce found the drawers empty. He set his cartons on top of the desk and began taking out his belongings and stacking files and documents in some sort of manageable order.

He would hang his diplomas and framed recognitions on the wall behind the desk. Research materials and empty file folders waiting for paperwork on players went into the plain gray file cabinet. He spread his playbooks and coaching charts on top of the desk, sat in the utilitarian metal chair and flipped through the material, deciding which formations would work for a coach starting up with a new team.

After a couple hours, he took a break to simply appreciate being where he'd always wanted to end up. He stared out a wide window that overlooked the field where, in a short time, he'd teach a bunch of raw players to become productive team members. One adult wearing shorts and a polo shirt stood on the sideline while two teens practiced pitching and catching a baseball in the center of the practice area.

Bryce spread his hands on the desktop and watched the interplay between the man and the boys. The man was obviously coaching.

Bryce understood the connection between a coach and his players. He understood what each meant to the other, how each player individually was a vital link to the success of the whole. How parents and family and friends contributed to what happened on the field.

He imagined Bucky Lowell in this office and figured he probably had had pictures of his family on this desk, images that comforted and supported him. Bryce had no pictures to put here, no wife or children to think of while he made decisions that affected so many lives and dreams. Audrey had taken his dream of kids away from him.

He sighed. Maybe, if the house deal went through, he'd get a dog, a photogenic one. And maybe, if he got really lucky, he'd marry again and have those couple of kids he'd always wanted. And then quite unexpectedly, an image of Rosalie came to his mind, the way she looked now—grown up but still with a youthful sultriness that took his breath despite the sadness of the past in her eyes. He shook his head. "Don't even go there, Bryce," he said. "The woman has made her attitude about you perfectly clear."

He left his office and wandered onto the practice field where the informal baseball session was still going on. The adult waved him over and stuck out his hand when Bryce approached. "Coach Benton," the man said. "Welcome to Whistler Creek. Or, welcome back I should say."

Bryce shook hands. "Thanks. It's been a long time."

"I'm Ted Fanning, baseball coach," the man said. "This will be my third year on the faculty."

"Nice to meet you." Bryce shielded his eyes and looked at the boys on the field. "I guess those are a couple of your stars?"

"That's right." He pointed. "Watch that pitcher. He'll knock your socks off."

Bryce observed the kid wind up and let loose with a curveball that seemed good enough to have been computer generated. "Wow. The kid's good."

"You bet he is." Coach Fanning cupped his hands around his mouth. "Let's see a fastball, Danny!"

The boy obliged and Bryce whistled in appreciation. "Damn. That pitch had to be nearly eighty miles an hour."

Fanning grinned. "I've clocked him at eighty-two. And how about that accuracy? The catcher barely has to move his arm. And the best thing is, I don't have to worry about the kid's dedication. Here it is, off-season, and he practically begs me for extra practice time."

Bryce continued to watch the phenom pitcher with mounting admiration. "How old is he?"

"Hard to believe, but he's only going to be a freshman this year." Again the grin. "I'll have him four more years. A coach's dream."

Yeah, and definite quarterback material. Bryce couldn't help fantasizing about seeing the kid in a football practice jersey. He'd already determined that the quarterback spot on the Wildcats would be up for grabs at the end of the current season. And he had no good prospect coming up the ranks. Unless…

"Ah, tell me something, Coach," he said.

"Sure thing."

"Do you think this kid might be interested in playing football along with baseball?"

Fanning's smile faded. "You're not thinking of taking my player, are you?"

"I wouldn't put it that way," Bryce said. "Just thought maybe he could do both."

Fanning scratched his head. "You're seeing him in a quarterback spot, aren't you?"

"He's got the arm for it."

Fanning thought a moment. "The seasons don't overlap. And he's certainly dedicated enough to go through additional training…."

Bryce sensed a "but" on the tip of Fanning's tongue. He waited. "So what is it? You don't want to share him?"

"I don't want a football injury affecting his pitching arm. And…"

"And what?" Bryce said.

"I know this kid's mother, and I don't think she'd be in favor of him playing football. She thinks it's dangerous."

Bryce didn't see that as a big problem. He'd persuaded reluctant parents into getting over football phobias before. "I'd talk to her," he said.

"You could try, but she's also a stickler for grades."

"Is the kid smart enough to handle the load of schoolwork and two sports?"

"I suppose, but this mom is a special case." Fanning's expression became wary. "She's going to be a hard sell, and I ought to know. I'm kind of dating her."

He announced the end of the practice session and Bryce kept his sights on the pitcher as the boys crossed the field. "Never hurts to ask though, does it?" he said to Ted.

"Go ahead. Talk to him."

Fanning put his hand on the boy's shoulder. "Nice workout, fellas. By the way, this is Whistler Creek's new football coach, boys. Coach Benton."

The teen who'd been catching Danny's pitches said hi and excused himself to head for the showers. Danny remained. He wiped his palm on his shorts and shook hands with Bryce. He was tall, only a couple inches shorter than Bryce. Definitely tall enough to fit the bill as QB. And there could still be a growth spurt in his future.

"I've heard about you," Danny said.

"And I've been watching you," Bryce said. "Good pitching style you've developed there."

Danny kicked a clod of dirt with his cleat. "Thanks."

Fanning looked from one to the other. "As a matter of fact, Danny, Coach here was wondering if you might be interested in playing for the football team."

The boy's eyes widened. "Really?"

"Well, we've been kicking the idea around," Bryce said. "There would have to be try-outs…."

The instantaneous enthusiasm faded from the boy's eyes. "I don't know how my mom would like the idea. Her brother…"

Danny paused, and a fifteen-year-old pain coiled in Bryce's gut. "Who is your mother, Danny?"

"She teaches at the high school," he said. "You…ah, you know her. Miss Campano, the English teacher."

Bryce could only gawk at Danny as if the kid had suddenly sprouted a second head. "You're Rosalie's son?" he repeated needlessly.

"Yeah."

Damn. Bryce's goal of nabbing the ideal quarterback suddenly didn't even seem a remote possibility. Of course Rosie wouldn't want her kid playing football. Of course she wouldn't want him playing for Bryce.

He walked Fanning a few steps away from Danny and spoke so only the coach could hear. "Do you know my connection to Rosalie's brother?" he asked.

"I've heard, but I don't want to get in the

middle of this." Fanning rubbed his hand over the back of his neck. "History can sure come back to bite you in the ass, can't it, Coach?"

Bryce realized he must look witless. He tried to smile at Danny Campano. "Nice meeting you, Danny," he said. "I'll see you around."

As he walked back to the athletic center, Bryce wondered how fortune could be so fickle. Show him a shining future star and then snuff it out behind a giant rain cloud. But what bothered him just as much was why he kept thinking about what Fanning had said about Rosalie. "I ought to know. I'm kind of dating her."

When Rosalie pulled into the high school lot, she immediately noticed the familiar tricked-out black pickup parked under the shade of an old oak tree.

"Great," she muttered to herself and chose a spot several spaces away. She backed in, turned off her engine and looked at her watch. A little before noon. If Danny was on time, a rarity when he was practicing, she'd see him sprinting across the practice field in just a few minutes. Hopefully they would be on their way home before Bryce returned to his truck.

Unfortunately the male figure she saw moments later wasn't Danny. Even from a distance, Rosalie recognized the features of the man who had been her childhood friend, her teenage companion and her eventual heartthrob. She lowered her sunglasses and stared, allowing herself the guilty pleasure of enjoying the natural grace of his walk, the confident swagger in his step. She smirked to herself. The man was still just too darned sexy for his own good.

She couldn't look at Bryce without remembering that morning after the prom and the scent of peaches mingling with his crisp, clean aftershave. She couldn't look at him without recalling the first mind-blowing kiss in the orchard, the first time his hands teased tingles of pleasure out of her eager young body. The first time he... She squeezed her eyes shut.

As always, the most tender memory of all was obliterated by the image of her brother unconscious on the ground, the sound of her own sobs and the cry of anguish from Bryce's lips.

Her senses on overdrive and her emotions on edge, she urged herself to stay in control. She had to expect to see Bryce often. She'd managed to run into him all three days since his surprise appearance Friday night. But she didn't want to see him again so soon, and not around Danny.

She slumped into her seat, grabbed a novel from the dashboard and opened to her bookmarked page. Even if Bryce realized she was in the car, perhaps he'd notice she was preoccupied and would politely get in his vehicle and leave.

Of course, she didn't read a word. She kept her gaze intent on the page, but when, a few agonizing minutes later, she heard Bryce's subtle step on the blacktop, any possibility of actually comprehending a sentence flew right out her open window. When she heard the truck door open, her face flushed all the way to the roots of her hair. When the door slammed, she released the breath she'd been holding. He was leaving. She frowned as she listened for the sound of his engine revving. Would she be thankful or disappointed?

Jeez, Rosalie, what is it that you want?

"Hey, Rosalie, I thought this was your car."

Her head snapped up. She swallowed a gasp and looked into the lenses of Bryce's aviator sunglasses. He hadn't left after all.

"I looked for you but didn't see you in your car until I got in my truck," he said, leaning into her window. "We seem to be running into each other everywhere these days."

She faked a grin. "Yeah. What are the odds in a town this size?"

He removed his glasses and pointed an earpiece toward the athletic building. "Oh, I met your boy today."

Her stomach plunged.

"Nice kid. Talented, too. He can really throw a baseball."

She pressed the flat of her hand over her abdomen—a protective gesture, but protective of what? The secret she still harbored? "That's what they tell me."

He put on the glasses and peered at her over the lenses. "And by the way, I met your other fella, too."

"My other fella?"

"Ted, the baseball coach. He says you and he are going out."

Wonderful. Rosalie had accepted less than a half-dozen dates with Ted this summer. She hadn't told anyone but Shelby, and intended to keep any relationship with a coworker private. She made up her mind to speak to him as soon as possible about being discreet. "Don't believe everything you hear," she said to Bryce.

"You're not dating him?"

"What I'm not doing is discussing this with you," she said, forcing what she hoped was a hint of casual humor into her answer.

"Okay." He stared over at the field and raised

his hand in a wave. "Looks like Danny's coming now."

Thank goodness. Now to get Bryce to his truck and Danny out of here before old home week continued. She heard the cell phone ringtone of Bruce Springsteen's "Born to Run" and glanced at Bryce's pocket. "Shouldn't you get that?" she asked.

He pulled his phone out and checked the caller ID. "Yeah, it's my real estate agent. We may have an answer to my offer on the Harbin place." He headed toward his truck. "See you, Rosie."

She took her first normal breath in minutes as she watched her son lope around the track toward the parking lot. Tall, olive-skinned, dark-haired. Danny looked more like his uncle Ricky than he did his father, a fact which allowed her confidence to return. If she could just keep Danny and Bryce apart, Bryce would never suspect.

Her mind flashed back to the two weeks after that first kiss in the peach orchard, the day a most unexpected jolt of love had zeroed in on her heart. Two weeks later, she still marveled that Bryce Benton, a boy she'd always loved in the way sisters do, was all at once the young man she now truly loved in the way sisters never could. There had been no doubt in Rosalie's mind that Bryce was the one. She couldn't wait until he made love to her. Bryce was worthy of her most precious gift, and she was determined to give it to him before he went off to college.

She went to her brother and confided her plan to him. He was the logical one in the Campano family to advise her since her father and mother would have had a tough time accepting that their daughter was planning to lose her virginity before the sacred bond of marriage.

Ricky had no such qualms. "You need to get on the Pill, Rosie," he told her. "That's what Beth uses. Guys really don't like to use condoms. And you don't have to worry about Bryce having something. I know for a fact that he's only been with one other girl."

The Pill. A prescription was needed, so she did what she believed was right even considering her parents' traditional views. With only two weeks until Bryce would leave for summer training at the University of Texas, she asked her mother to accompany her to the doctor's office. She believed Claudia would consent. After all, this was Bryce, and Claudia loved him, too.

Claudia staunchly refused to consent to birth control pills, saying Enzo would be horrified at this decision. She couldn't go against his wishes. Unfortunately for Rosalie, the family doctor wouldn't prescribe the pills otherwise. Coming up with a backup plan to try an out-of-area clinic on her own, Rosalie drove to Valdosta, thirty miles away. Once again the prescription was denied.

But Rosalie had promised Bryce that she would be on the Pill in time for the special night he'd planned when his parents were going to be out of town. So she went to the Benton home with only a flimsily wrapped foil package she'd discovered in the back of Ricky's nightstand drawer.

And then she didn't even offer the condom to Bryce. Too embarrassed at failing to get the pills. Too in love for the first time in her life. Too caught up in the passion of a moment that promised to fulfill all her preconceived notions about love and sex. Later, Rosalie wondered why she'd let those reasons lead her into having unprotected sex and trusting in the most fickle of outcomes.

Even then, everything might have worked out if only that football hadn't rocketed from Bryce's hand into Ricky's temple the very next day. If only Ricky hadn't died minutes later. Less than twenty-four hours after making love with Bryce, Rosalie lost her brother. The fear and hatred of football, which she'd experienced ever since that day, took root in her soul. And she knew her love for Bryce Benton would be forever tarnished.

"Hi, Mom. Sorry I'm late."

Danny hopped in the car and Rosalie switched

mental gears to be a mother again. "No problem," she said and started the car.

Danny slanted a gaze at her. "I think I've made a decision today," he said.

"Oh? What's that?"

She was heading out of the parking lot when Danny responded, and she very nearly ran into the majestic old oak tree that had recently shaded Bryce's truck.

"I'm going to try out for football."

Chapter Five

"You're a baseball player, that's why not."

Rosalie hated the petulant tone of her voice, but this argument had been going on with few interruptions since she and Danny had arrived home. Now, with Claudia in the living room watching TV, Rosalie and Danny washed the dinner dishes and returned once again to this bitter topic.

"That's no reason, Mom," Danny said.

"It will have to do. You've been playing baseball since you were four years old. That's almost eleven years. If you switch now you'll have to learn a whole new set of skills. You'll start to ignore the old ones."

"No, I won't. I can do both. Why can't I?"

"Look, Danny, I'm your mother, and…" She stopped herself before she slipped into using old clichés such as, "Because I said so." Or issuing edicts like the one she had gotten from her mother when Claudia had refused to sign for birth control pills. "Good girls don't have sex before marriage," Claudia had said, and though Rosalie believed her mother's belief to be outdated and unrealistic, she hadn't known any way to argue.

This was all Bryce's fault, putting ideas into Danny's head and making her look like the bad guy. She hung the dishcloth over the sink divider, took a deep, calming breath and looked at her son. "Honey, I am so proud of you, you know that. Look what you've accomplished by striving and practicing to become the best pitcher you can be. Why do you want to take the chance of messing up all your hard work?"

"I won't mess anything up. The two sports

don't happen at the same time. I can concentrate on each one during different seasons." He noisily stacked plates in the cupboard before turning to stare at her. "Mom, Coach Fanning doesn't care if I try out. If he doesn't, why should you?"

She squeezed her eyes shut and rubbed the lids, forcing herself to think rationally. Only this wasn't a rational situation. She knew it, and she suspected Danny did too, though he didn't know all the reasons why this was so difficult for her. After a moment, she pulled out a chair and gestured for him to sit. When he did, she sat opposite him at the table.

She folded her hands on top. "Danny, the simple truth is that I don't want you playing football. And you know why."

"Because of Uncle Ricky."

"Yes, that's right."

"Mom, I know he was your brother and all, but that's just crazy."

She jerked back in her chair and glared at him for a moment. His words stung, perhaps because they were too close to reality. It wasn't as if she hadn't known her fear of football was born of that one tragedy. She realized her feelings bordered on phobic, but she couldn't help it. She'd lost half her soul, half her heart that day. And since then, she'd researched every aspect of football-related brain trauma injuries trying to make sense of what happened to Ricky. And now, years later, she'd reached the conclusion that despite improvements in training and equipment, these types of injuries still occurred all too often. And many of them happened to quarterbacks, young men just like Ricky, just like Danny could be if she gave into his desires.

Danny looked down, resting his forehead in his hand. "I'm sorry, Mom. I shouldn't have said that."

"It's okay."

When he raised his face, his eyes—Bryce's blue eyes—shone with the same determination he'd exhibited all evening. Maybe he was sorry for calling her crazy, but he wasn't giving up.

"I know how you felt about Uncle Ricky," he said. "And I've heard all the stories about what a great kid he was. And also about what a great football player he was. Maybe I just want to be like him."

"You don't have to be like him," she said. *I don't want you to be.* "You couldn't be anyway. You're your own person, doing your own thing, making your name in a different way."

His gaze never wavered. "I know about the accident and how Coach Benton was involved. But, Mom, nobody in town blames Coach Benton for Uncle Ricky dying. It was a freak *accident.* That means it just happened, no one was at fault."

Logically she knew that. But emotionally she couldn't forget that day in the park, the day after she'd lost her virginity to Bryce. Many of her friends, recent Whistler Creek High School graduates, had met at the park, bringing picnic baskets filled with food and contraband beer hidden under napkins and poured discreetly into paper cups.

They'd all been celebrating, talking about their futures, the bright ones guys like Bryce and Ricky had with their scholarships and promises of easy rides at universities. Rosalie was happy for them though her own future was much different. Only a slightly above-average student, she hadn't earned a scholarship of any kind. Her parents wished they could send her to college, but the meager Campano family savings had to go to Ricky, the male of the family, the one whose education was most vital.

The Campano savings would go to Ricky's living expenses, the ones his scholarship wouldn't cover. Rosalie planned to work for a year, save her earnings so she could afford the tuition to follow her own ambition of becoming a teacher.

Though she sometimes questioned the way things had to be, she didn't resent Ricky because he would enjoy advantages she wouldn't have. It was spring. She was in love. Her future was bright and hopeful. Someday she would marry Bryce, and her focus would switch to being a good wife, something Claudia had prepared her for. Or maybe she could still go to college. She had options that day, only she didn't know that those options were about to be severely narrowed.

She spread out the picnic lunch she'd brought as Bryce and Ricky started goofing off, boasting about their athletic prowess as they often did. They picked up a football and began tossing it around, competing over whose throws went the farthest, whose control was better.

She could still hear Bryce bragging. "How about it, QB?" he'd said to his best friend. "Go out for a long one and I'll show you that a lowly wide receiver can spiral a bullet as good as any quarterback."

Ricky challenged him with the macho insolence that had characterized both boys during their years playing high school football. "Give it your best shot," he'd hollered, sprinting down the open meadow. "I bet you don't even get close to me."

Bryce waited until Ricky was in place and

then let loose with a long, spinning missile that streaked toward its target. What happened next tested the beliefs of everyone who witnessed the event. The ball headed straight for Ricky's head. And Ricky stood there legs apart, arms at his sides, unflinching, fifty yards away. His laughter carried across that field as if he didn't have a care in the world. As if he didn't think Death could ever touch him.

But it did. When the tip of the ball caught him in the right temple, Ricky dropped and didn't move. He was pronounced dead at the hospital before his body was even taken from the ambulance.

The doctors offered theories to his grieving family. The concussion he'd sustained during the football season had left him susceptible to further complications though the chances of any fatal injury had been extremely remote—almost unheard of. The ball had to hit him just so. The brain had to have been jolted at just the right angle of impact with the skull. A freakish thing all around.

Every day for a full year afterward, and nearly every day since, Rosalie had asked the unanswerable questions. Why did Bryce have to throw that pass? Why didn't Ricky put up his hand? Why didn't he duck? The simple, horrible, tragic truth was that it didn't have to happen.

"Mom, are you listening to me?"

Danny's voice and the pain of her fingernails digging into her palm brought Rosalie back from her dark place. She forced herself to extend her fingers and looked at her son. "Sorry. What did you say?"

"So is it okay with you if I try out?"

A freak accident. Unfortunately they happened all the time in one form or another. The phrase her son had just used appeared in news headlines and at funerals as explanations for the unreasonable. Freak accidents weren't so rare when they happened in your family. She exhaled. "Let me sleep on it, Danny. You're going with Grandma to Benton's in the morning, right?"

"Yeah."

"I have to go to the Board of Education office to pick up the new American Lit textbook. We'll see each other later in the day."

"And you'll tell me then?"

She muzzled her impatience. "I'll try, but don't put me on a deadline, Danny. This isn't an easy decision for me."

His glare was defiant, his jaw muscles clenched. She couldn't remember ever seeing his face like that before.

He stood. "I'm going to my room."

"Okay."

She remained at the table after he'd left, thinking about what she would do next. When minutes passed, Claudia came into the kitchen, Dixie trailing behind her. "How did it go?" she asked.

"I'm not sure it could have been worse."

"What now?"

Rosalie reached out and patted the dog's head. "What's the best thing a person can do when faced with a problem, Mom?"

Claudia leaned against the sink and folded her arms. "Face it, I guess."

"That's right, and that's what I'm going to do. I have a problem, and the sensible thing, the *only* thing I can think to do is go to the source."

Claudia slowly shook her head. "Oh, boy."

The next morning when she was alone in the house, Rosalie dialed up the Benton home. She hadn't called the number in almost fifteen years but she still remembered it.

"Hello?"

"Mrs. Benton. This is Rosalie Campano."

There was a pause before Marjorie said, "Rosalie. What a surprise. What can I do for you?"

"I need to speak to Bryce. Is he there?"

"No. He's actually out your way at some piece of property he has it in his mind to buy. He's meeting with an inspector."

"Thank you. Maybe I'll run over there." No maybe about it.

"Do you want Bryce's cell phone number?"

"No. I don't need it." She started to say goodbye and then thought better of her hasty decision. "Actually, Mrs. Benton, I will take that phone number."

She scribbled it on a piece of scrap paper and tucked it in the pocket of her jeans. Couldn't hurt to let him know she was on her way. But she didn't call until she was almost there. He was bound to know what this was about, and she didn't want him to have time to build up a defense for his actions.

"Hello."

"Bryce? This is Rosalie."

"Well, Rosalie, how are...?"

"Your mother gave me your number. I understand you're at the Harbin place."

"I am."

"I'd like to stop by. I can be there in just a few minutes."

"I'll wait for you. Come on over."

He sat on the front porch steps and considered Rosalie's reason for coming to see him. She'd sounded pissed, so he could only assume this was about what happened between her son and him. He smiled to himself despite his anxiety over her impending visit. Hell, Rosie had been pissed at him since he'd been back, probably had been for fifteen years, so why was he surprised?

He stared down the overgrown drive, watching for her little red car. He was not going to let her put this whole issue on his shoulders. Even her boyfriend, Fanning, agreed that Danny could handle two sports. Besides it wasn't a done deal. Bryce had told the kid there would have to be tryouts.

"Hey, Coach!"

Bryce stood when he heard the inspector's voice and walked to the side of the house. Mr. Gibbons stared down at him from the roof where he was holding onto the chimney. "How's everything look up there?" Bryce asked.

"Not bad. This roof's been replaced at least once over the years. You ought to get four or five more years out of her."

"That's good."

"Hold the ladder for me. I'm coming down."

Bryce steadied the ladder while the older man gingerly stepped to the ground. Gibbons picked up his clipboard, made a notation and said, "That completes the inspection. I found one toilet not flushing like it should, and you need to replace the pipes under the kitchen sink, but otherwise this house should outlast you and me both."

"Just what I wanted to hear," Bryce said, scanning the report. He could easily manage the few repairs listed. When he heard the sound of a car engine, he was suddenly anxious to get Mr. Gibbons on his way. "What do I owe you?"

"Three-hundred-fifty dollars. I'll send a bill out to your parents' place and you can mail me a check."

"Fair enough."

Rosalie's compact Ford braked in front of the house, sending up a plume of gravel dust. "You got company," Gibbons said.

Bryce flinched as Rosalie got out of the car and slammed the door. "Yeah, but I don't think it's the welcoming committee."

Gibbons chuckled. "No. It's Rosalie." He walked over toward the car and spoke to her. "Your mom got any acorn squash at the stand?"

Rosalie indicated that she did.

"I'll stop on my way back to town. Feel like baking some squash with butter and cinnamon on it." He turned to Bryce and offered his hand. "Good luck this season. My wife and I never miss a game."

Bryce thanked him and waited until Gibbons had turned his truck toward the drive and headed away. Then he spoke to Rosalie. "Just had an inspection on the house. Looks like I'm going through with the purchase."

She shielded her eyes from a spear of sunlight and gave his new possession the once-over. "Actually, the place looks pretty good, considering it's stood vacant for a few years."

Encouraged by her interest, he held up the

key the Realtor had given him and said, "You want to see the inside?"

"Maybe some other time. I'm on a tight schedule this morning."

Inexplicably disappointed, he forced an indifferent shrug. He'd tried to work up a good head of steam about this visit, but Rosalie looked so darned good with just a hint of makeup and her thick, dark hair pulled back in clips. Now all he wanted to do was coax a smile out of her.

"You look nice," he said, realizing the comment was more than a little understated. She looked great in formfitting black jeans, a red V-neck sleeveless sweater and black sandals that framed painted toenails.

Sexy. He pushed the word from his mind.

"I'm on my way to the school board office."

"We can sit on the steps," he said. "I swept the dust off them."

"I don't need to sit to say what's on my mind."

He tried to hide his frustration behind a smile. "So I take it this isn't a social call?"

"You know it isn't." She exhaled. "Bryce, you've created a firestorm around my house."

"In what way?" But he knew damn well playing dumb would only postpone the inevitable confrontation.

"You had no right to try and coax Danny into playing football."

Now she was just being unreasonable. And incorrect. "First of all, I didn't try to coax him. Your boyfriend introduced us…"

"Quit calling him my boyfriend. It's juvenile."

"Okay. The *baseball coach,* Ted Fanning, whom I believe you know, introduced us. I'd noticed Danny's talent, and football naturally came up in the conversation."

"And you didn't see a problem with that?"

"I didn't know he was your son then."

"Fine. But when you did discover he was my son, did that make a difference?"

"I was concerned about it, yes." He could have let his answer drop there, but he didn't.

"Because of the way you obviously still feel about me and what happened."

If he'd expected a denial, hoped for it, he didn't get it.

"Still, you didn't discourage him," she said. "As I started to tell you before, you had no right…."

It occurred to Bryce that a good coach knows to concentrate on both offense and defense in equal parts. Now was the time to put that theory into practice and initiate a little offense of his own. He'd vowed that Rosalie wasn't going to walk all over him, but so far, he'd let her.

He folded his arms over his chest and interrupted her. "Here's something that may have slipped your mind as far as my rights as a football coach are concerned, Rosalie. It is indeed my right, as well as my *job,* to put together the best team I can—for this school, this community and especially for the guys who'll be playing for me. That means that any young man who shows the potential to make that happen is fair game."

Her eyes blazed. "Not my son. And I don't have to remind you why."

"Of course you don't. But come on, Rosalie. Do you really believe that some freakish twist of fate in our history might repeat itself? What are the chances of that happening?"

"What were the chances of it happening the first time?"

He paused, took a deep breath and continued with what he hoped was a more sympathetic tone. Seeing her son at a crossroad in his life, a path that brought back painful memories, had to be hard for Rosie to accept. Hell, it was for him. But Bryce felt he had to try. For himself, sure. His future depended on the job he would do in Whistler Creek. But he suddenly realized that he needed to change Rosalie's opinion of him for a kid he hardly knew. One who could pay the price for a tragedy from the past, a tragedy young Danny Campano had nothing to do with.

He reached out, wrapped his hand around her arm. She didn't back away, and he was encouraged that maybe he'd touched some part of her he used to know.

"We're assuming way too much here, Rosalie," he said. "In truth, Danny seemed pretty casual about the whole thing. He said you might not go for it."

"And he was right."

Bryce dropped his hand to his side and smiled, just a little. "Anyway, I couldn't tell if he was enthusiastic about the idea, or even all that interested."

"Now we know he is indeed interested." Her toe tapped in the dust. "But what's your point?"

"My point is, that we should wait until we even know if Danny is going to try out. Maybe he'll change his mind." Bryce hunched his shoulders, attempting to affect a casual attitude of his own. "Hell, Rosalie, maybe he won't even make the team."

Her eyes widened. "That's it," she said. "He

won't make the team. You can stop this from ever…"

He put his hand up. "Don't go there, Rosalie. You can't expect me…"

"But I am expecting just that, Bryce. Promise me you won't put Danny on the team, especially not as quarterback."

He blew out a long breath and looked at the ground before focusing on her again. Her facial features were expectant, hopeful. And he had to dash that hope.

"I won't promise that, Rosalie. You're asking me to make a decision when I haven't even seen your kid throw a football."

"I'm asking you to do the decent thing, Bryce. For my son, for me, for my family. Haven't we suffered enough from this damn game? Do the Campanos have to give even more?"

Her eyes glistened. Her shoulders trembled. And he suddenly remembered that morning with peach blossoms, chilled champagne and the kiss that changed his life. His hands flexed at his sides, and he clenched them to keep from reaching out to her and pulling her to him.

Once he'd been able to make her laugh, make her tremble when his hands moved over her. Any thought he may have had in the back of his mind that he and Rosie might start over didn't matter now. She couldn't look at him with any emotion other than regret.

He wished he could make the grief go away for her. But it was too deep, too intense, too personal. After all, images of that fateful day still lingered with him every day, still made his heart ache with the unfairness of it all. And now, he realized how those same images haunted Rosie, his Rosie, the last girl he'd ever meant to hurt, but whose spirit he'd killed, the woman who still suffered from that one inexplicable, horrible moment. He couldn't make it better for her. He couldn't give her what she wanted or needed.

It was all just so damned sad.

"So you won't keep him off the team?" she said.

"Rosie, don't ask me to do that…."

"But I am asking."

He just waited, stared at her.

She sniffed, rubbed a finger under her eye. "I have to go."

"Rosalie, I'm sorry it happened. I've said it before, a hundred times it seems, but it's still true. I loved Ricky like a brother."

She bit hard on her bottom lip. "So did I, Bryce. So did I." She straightened her spine and headed toward her car. "I told Danny I'd give him my answer tonight about the tryout."

"What are you going to tell him?" Bryce asked.

She opened her car door and looked at him before getting in. "I haven't the faintest idea."

Chapter Six

Once the dinner dishes were put away, Rosalie took a tumbler of iced tea to the front porch. Dixie followed her out the screen door and settled by the steps. Claudia, her reading glasses perched on her nose, was deftly stitching French knots on a table scarf. Rosalie sat in the rocking chair next to her and looked at the handiwork. "That's pretty. Where are you going to use it?"

Claudia shrugged. "I don't know. I've already got so many. I'll probably give it to someone for Christmas."

"Anyone would be glad to have it."

Claudia twined thread around her needle and poked it into the linen. "Nice night."

Rosalie rocked. "Hmm."

Several minutes of silence went by before Claudia looked at her daughter, sighed and said, "He's fifteen, Rosie. It's not unusual for teenage boys to have plans for dinner that don't include his family."

"I know. It's just unusual for Danny."

"It's not like he didn't call," Claudia said.

Rosalie's right foot set the old rocker pitching at a faster pace. "What did he say exactly, Mom?"

"He said he was eating out with Greg and he'd be home by eight."

Rosalie stared over the lawn to the road. "It's almost eight now. I wouldn't worry except that I know he's pissed at me."

"And this is his attempt to punish you? By giving you a night off from cooking?"

"Maybe."

Claudia put her sewing on the floor by her chair. "So what have you decided?"

Rosalie frowned. "I haven't yet." She felt her mother's stare but refused to look directly at her. "This is hard for me, Mom. I don't want him playing football."

"I think you've made that clear."

"And you don't agree?"

Claudia reached over and put her hand on Rosalie's arm. "I don't want him hurt, Rosie...."

Sensing her mother was on her side, Rosalie said, "So you do understand. That's all I'm trying to do. Keep Danny from getting hurt."

Claudia smiled. "You didn't let me finish. There's more than one way for a boy his age to be hurt. There's the physical way. And then there's the emotional way."

Rosalie stood, walked to the edge of the porch and wrapped her hands around the railing. "What are you trying to say, Mom?"

"I'm saying that you can't keep a safety net under that boy his whole life."

"I'm not doing that!"

"Oh, no? You've got to let him breathe, honey, even if it goes against what you want. You've got to let him experience things, make his own decisions."

Rosalie stared up at the porch ceiling. "I can't believe you aren't supporting me in this. After everything we've been through. It's almost like you forgot…."

She turned around and saw the hurt in her mother's eyes. "I'm sorry. I didn't mean that."

"It's all right. Everyone's nerves are on edge around here."

"So, if you were me, you'd let him play?"

Claudia waited a moment and said, "I don't know that you have any choice."

"That's certainly not true. As far as I know, there are still papers that have to be signed for a kid to play sports in this county. Parental consent forms. I could always refuse."

Claudia chewed on her bottom lip. "About that…"

Rosalie returned to the rocker and sat. "Mom, you know something. What is it?"

"Danny talked to me about this."

Feeling inexplicably hurt, Rosalie said, "He came to you?"

Claudia nodded. "He's torn, Rosie. He wants to play but he doesn't want to have to fight you to do it." A few uncomfortable ticks of the clock went by before Claudia said, "He appears to have come up with a plan."

"What plan?"

Claudia gazed over the lawn a moment before confessing. "He asked me about his father."

"Oh, God." Rosalie squeezed her eyes shut as if that would block out the rest of this conversation. "What did he say?"

"He asked me if I knew where his father was."

An image of the Harbin place swam before Rosalie's eyelids. There was no way she could let Danny find out his father would soon be living less than a mile away. Fighting a shiver of dread, she opened her eyes. "What did you tell him?"

"You know I don't like to lie."

"Mom, for Pete's sake, what did you say?"

"I said I didn't know where his father was at that particular time. That was true. I didn't know where Bryce was this morning when Danny and I talked."

Rosalie placed her hand over her pounding heart. "Okay. Then what?"

"He asked if his father lived nearby. I said the last I heard he was fairly close."

"Oh, jeez." Rosalie swallowed around a lump in her throat. "He's going to try to contact him, I just know it."

"Looks that way, honey."

"He thinks he can ask his father to sign the papers if I won't." Rosalie took a minute to let the consequences of Danny's plan sink in. "Mom, this is what I've always feared. You know it's not just the football thing I'm against, although that would be enough. It's Bryce. I don't want Danny getting close to him. I don't want either one of them to know what I did."

"That's your pain, Rosalie. You have to bear

it. You can't inflict the regrets of your past on to Danny."

"But I can't tell Danny the truth!"

"Then consider what I told you as a warning. You may have to sign those papers or come up with a darned good story about who Danny's father is. I think it's going to come down to that."

Rosalie choked back a sob. "Everything was so simple when Danny was little. Now it's all threatening to come unraveled. How did I get myself into this mess?"

Claudia patted her hand. "It wasn't just you, Rosie. All of us, your dad, me, Roland and Marjorie, we all played a part. We influenced you probably more than we should have."

"But it seemed like the right decision at the time."

"Yes, maybe. But now I'm not so sure."

A painful memory flooded Rosalie's mind. Fifteen years ago. Five people sitting around the Bentons' dining room table, discussing Rosalie's future and the future of her unborn child. Now that she thought about that night, Rosalie realized that Claudia had been silent through most of the conversation, letting her husband speak for the family. The adults had all had strong opinions, each wanting what they thought was best for the baby. But in the end, Rosalie's desires prevailed. Her baby would be loved and cared for. She wouldn't be forced into a marriage with the man who'd been responsible for her family's tragedy. And Bryce, well, she believed he benefited more than anyone. He could achieve his dreams of playing football and maybe even go on to a pro team. But now, thinking back, Rosalie wondered why her mother had hardly spoken.

She needed to know. "Mom? I have to ask you about that night at the Benton house…."

She paused when Dixie ran down the steps, her tail wagging.

Claudia stared at the drive. "Not now, Rosalie. Danny's home."

Danny got out of his friend's car, waved goodbye and climbed the steps to the porch.

Getting down on one knee, he patted Dixie. Then he looked up at his mother and said, "So what's your answer, Mom? Can I see Coach tomorrow?"

Blunt, to the point. Rosalie wasn't ready. She managed a small smile. "Come in the house with me, Danny."

He stood. "What for? Is this something you can't say in front of Grandma?"

Rosalie glanced at her mother who had taken a sudden keen interest in her sewing again. Rosalie was still reeling from Claudia's warning and decided it best that she talk to Danny alone. "I thought you might want to go to the kitchen. Maybe you're hungry."

"I just came from Applebee's, Mom."

"Well, I want more iced tea, so come inside." She opened the door, waited for Danny to go ahead of her into the kitchen. After pouring a glass of tea she hoped would cool her parched throat, she pulled out two chairs at the table. "Sit, honey."

He plopped his rear end on the seat of a chair

and slouched defiantly. Rosalie sat across from him and took a sip to stall for time. Looking at her son's face, his expression a cross between determination and expectation, she felt her resolve slipping away.

Danny cleared his throat. "So, Mom, can I?"

She wrapped her hands around the glass. "I've been thinking about this all day. You know how I feel."

"Yeah." He leaned forward and put his elbows on the table. "And you know how I feel. And I've been talking to Greg about this. I don't think you have the right to keep me from doing what I want."

She felt the hair on her nape prickle. "You're wrong about that," she said, trying to tamp a spike of anger at his macho defiance. "I have to sign the consent forms for you to play."

He exhaled, stared down at the tabletop between his arms. Rosalie braced herself for a conversation about Danny's father, but instead he said, "You wouldn't keep me from doing this, Mom. You're not like that."

No, she wasn't. At least she hadn't been "like that" at any other time in Danny's life. But, then, he'd never asked to do something so contrary to everything she'd experienced and believed in. His decisions had never caused her chest to constrict with pain. She'd never been threatened with having the wits scared out of her. Nor had she been forced to face her past in such an agonizing way.

She looked at Danny, the brightest light of her life, the sweet compensation that had given purpose to her days after Ricky died. The child of the boy she'd once loved with her whole being. She'd never denied her son anything he really wanted. But now he was asking her to rip her own heart out.

He raised his face, drew in a deep breath and shot her a look so full of hope and confidence in her that her eyes misted with tears.

"Mom, please."

And she couldn't deny him now, either. Not tonight. She closed her eyes for a moment and thought of Bryce. He knew how she felt. He understood what she had asked of him yesterday. Maybe he would do the decent thing. She could hope. She could buy time. Maybe tomorrow…

Her shoulders slumped. She licked her dry lips. And then she said, "You can go talk to him…."

Danny leaped from the chair and pumped his fist in the air. "Mom, you're the best."

His enthusiasm only made her fear grow. He was so like his uncle. "I only said you could talk to him. Just talk. We don't know how this is going to turn out. You might not make the team."

He opened the refrigerator door, grabbed the gallon of milk and poured a tall glass. "Sure, that's possible."

"You might change your mind."

He gulped half the glass. "No. If I make the team, I'll play. This is what I want, Mom." He set down the glass and looked at her, perhaps realizing he should rein in his enthusiasm. "What I mean is… I want this *and* baseball.

I want them both, and I can do both. I know I can."

"Just don't get your hopes up," she said, knowing that was exactly what *she* was doing. Putting her hope in Bryce. Putting her hope in her son's failure. What kind of a mother did that?

"Will you drive me to school in the morning, Mom? Coach should be there early."

Her neck felt stiff, the movement awkward, but nevertheless she nodded.

Bryce sat in his office early Thursday morning with files on his returning players spread across the desktop. He was determined to read Bucky's recommendations on each kid before practice officially started in a week. When the players showed up on the field, Bryce would be ready to evaluate each one's strengths and weaknesses and form his own opinions.

Unfortunately this morning, he hadn't been able to concentrate. He'd been thinking about Rosalie since she came to the Harbin place two days ago. He'd finally admitted to himself that he'd had expectations when he had returned to Whistler Creek. Expectations about Rosalie. Did he think they could take up where they'd left off as teenagers? No. But still some part of him thought, hoped, a connection was possible.

Even though Bryce had dated a lot of girls, even though he'd been married, he'd never forgotten the gut-wrenching punch of that morning in the peach orchard. He had kissed his childhood friend and realized in that moment he might have been in love with Rosie Campano for most of his life. No other kiss had ever compared with that one.

After Ricky's funeral, where Rosalie had sat as quiet as a statue, her eyes blank, her lips moving in silent prayer, Bryce had tried to contact her. He'd called her home, left messages. When he'd gone away to college, he had written her letters, too many to count. She'd never answered any of them. He wondered if she even opened them. Years later, after his divorce, the world was connecting via email and social networks. He'd thought about sending

Rosalie messages, casual, cheerful how-'ya-doing-old-buddy one-liners, but he'd deleted each one before sending.

He'd followed her life through the contacts he still maintained in Whistler Creek. His mother told him that Rosalie had had a baby about a year after Bryce left town. Crushed under the weight of a broken heart, Bryce stopped writing her letters. Rosalie had gone forward with her life, found someone else to help her through her grief. Later he had heard that she'd graduated college and accepted a job at Whistler Creek High School. And Bryce moved forward, as well.

But now he'd seen her, and those old emotions had flared anew. Bryce didn't want to be done with Rosalie, but she didn't want any part of him. And now this damn problem with her kid. Maybe Rosalie had gotten through to Danny. Maybe she'd put her foot down and refused to grant him permission to try out. That would leave Bryce out of this whole sticky situation among the three of them. If Rosalie denied her son's wishes, though, it would be a shame—the kid had talent. But at least the moral decision would be out of Bryce's hands.

He opened a file and started reading the stats on the Wildcat punter. He had a job to do. One week until practice, one week until the expedited closing on his house. He'd stay busy. He'd put Danny out of his mind.

He looked up when he heard a rapping on the frame of his door. "Excuse me, Coach," Danny Campano said. "Can I talk to you?"

Danny could have been any of a countless number of young men Bryce had worked with, beginning as a high school assistant coach and eventually working up to college ball. His medium-length dark hair had that just-tumbled-out-of-bed messiness. He wore a gray T-shirt with faded navy letters identifying it as coming from the Wildcats Athletic Department. Loose-fitting nylon shorts stopped just above strong calves. Large, slightly worn black-and-white sneakers completed the image.

Only this wasn't any boy. This was Rosalie's son who stood in the doorway exhibiting a tentative confidence. His fists clenched at his sides, his posture ramrod straight, his shoulders squared.

Bryce started to stand, an involuntary reaction, but quickly settled back in his chair. "Ah, sure, Danny, come on in." He indicated the chair across the desk and Danny sat.

"What can I do for you?" Bryce asked, his heart beating rapidly.

Danny clasped his hands between his knees. "I came to try out, to show you what I can do. I want to be on the football team."

"I see." Bryce stalled for time. How had this come about? "I never asked you the other day, have you had any experience in this sport?"

"No, sir, unless you count all the games I've gone to and watched on TV. But I've studied the game, and I always wanted to play. Even when I was a kid."

Bryce knew the answer to his next question, but he asked it anyway. "So why haven't you?"

Danny's eyes darted to the window for an instant before he leveled a serious gaze on Bryce again. "I guess I just always assumed I was a baseball player. I like baseball, but I think I'd like football even more."

Bryce leaned back in his chair, threaded his hands over his waist. There was no getting around the topic that hung in the air between them, and he had to broach it. "Danny, does your mother know you're here today?"

His head nodded slightly. "Yeah, she's cool with it."

"She is?"

"Yes, Coach. In fact she dropped me off. She knows I'm coming to see you."

"She knows you're trying out?"

"Yes, sir."

"For the position of quarterback?"

"Yep."

Bryce was pretty good at reading kids, judging their body language. Danny didn't seem to be lying, but what had happened at the Campano house to make Rosalie get behind her son's decision? Bryce didn't want to leave any half-truths between himself and Danny so he asked the question which would address the last barrier. "Danny, do you know the history I share with your family, specifically what happened with your uncle?"

"Of course, Coach. Everybody knows about the pass, the accident." He paused before adding, "And nobody blames you."

Yeah, nobody but Rosalie. "That's good to know, but the only person I'm worried about right now is you. If this works out…and I'm not saying it will. I haven't even seen you throw a football yet…."

"I know, Coach. But I'm a hard worker and a fast learner."

"Maybe you are, but more than brains and guts is needed in this game. There has to be a fair amount of raw talent."

Danny nodded. "All I want is a chance, like any other guy. Just an opportunity to fill a spot on the team."

Bryce exhaled, a full deep release of the breaths that had seemed locked in his lungs the past few minutes. "I'll give you that chance, but a coach and his players have to develop a bond of trust, respect. You have to listen to me and my staff, work with us and with the other team members. If, for any reason, you don't think you can trust me… If anything that happened in the past might cause you to question my authority, my judgment, my decisions to act in the best interest of the Wildcats, then we couldn't work together."

Danny shook his head vigorously. "That won't happen, Coach."

"All right, then. Let's see what you can do." He motioned Danny out of the office. "Footballs are in the weight room lockers. Take out a half dozen."

Danny stopped at the door. "You want me to pad up?"

Bryce smiled. "No need. But I do want you to warm up. Do some stretching exercises, push-ups, sit-ups. Use the equipment for a half hour and I'll meet you on the field."

"Yes, sir."

When he'd gone, Bryce picked up his telephone and called a number he'd committed to memory. Gratified when the familiar gravelly voice answered, he said, "Cappy, you busy?"

"Not doing a thing. What do you need?"

"I'd like you to come to the field house and evaluate a new kid who's trying out for backup QB. Run him through a few drills and then I'll meet you there and we'll discuss his possibilities."

"I'm on my way."

Twenty minutes later Bryce introduced Gordon Capps to Danny. "Gordon played backup quarterback for the Atlanta Falcons from '78 to '84," Bryce explained.

"I know who you are, Mr. Capps," Danny said, shaking hands with the gray-haired man. "I used to have a football card of you."

"We were lucky enough to get him to volunteer to be our offensive coordinator," Bryce said. "He's going to be a big asset this season, and if you want a chance to play for the Wildcats, you'll have to first impress Cappy."

Bryce sent the two males onto the field with a bag of footballs and a stack of orange cones to use as targets. Bryce had known Cappy for years and trusted his judgment, much more than he trusted his own with regard to Danny. Cappy would give him an honest evaluation of Danny's potential. Without the bias of a painful past or a conflicted present, he'd give the kid the fair shot that Bryce might not.

Bryce went back into his office and opened a window. He watched Cappy work with Danny, gesturing, demonstrating, shouting instructions. "Fingers on the stitches," he called to Danny. "Set your feet, son. Your toes have to be aimed at the receiver before you release the ball."

After two hours, Bryce went outside, watched the final minutes of the session, and drew his own conclusion. Either Danny was a natural athlete, or Cappy was a training genius. No matter, Danny was going to be on the Wildcats team.

Cappy gave Danny instructions to keep practicing and came over to the sidelines. "The kid's good, Bryce."

"I can see that."

"Any coach would be excited to have him as first string QB, but as a backup for the coming season, he'll be the insurance policy you need."

An image of Rosalie—the way she had looked at his new house—barreled into his mind. Her words haunted him now. *He won't make the team. You can stop this.* Did she still think Bryce might keep the kid from playing? Had she changed her mind? If so, at what cost? Danny had said his mom was behind his decision, so at this point, with nothing else to go on, no contact from Rosalie, Bryce had to believe him.

Cappy cleared his throat, and Bryce realized his mind had wandered. "I want to run the kid through a couple sprint drills," Cappy said. "After that, should I tell Danny you want to see him?"

"Yeah. I'll go inside to get my stopwatch. We'll talk out here."

Bryce went into the field house and headed down the hall to his office. And stopped cold when he saw Rosalie peering in the window of his door. Her face was flushed. She had on workout clothes and sneakers. Her hair was pulled back in a ponytail, and she looked so much like his Rosie that his heart clenched. And fifteen years melted away.

Chapter Seven

"Rosalie."

She stepped away from the door and turned as if she'd been caught doing something she shouldn't. Why did the mere sound of Bryce's voice make her feel guilty?

Her name coming from his mouth sounded scratchy, as if he'd had a hard time forcing out the word. His gaze was fixed on her, and he approached slowly. Suddenly conscious of her bare midriff below her spandex tank, she crossed her arms at her waist. This wasn't the scenario she'd planned when she got out of her car and walked to the athletic building. She'd hoped to see Danny waiting by the exit, and she'd drag him back to the car with a reprimand about how he'd missed the pickup time they'd agreed upon.

Yet, as she looked at Bryce, his face and arms tanned from the Georgia sun, his waist still slender and legs still nicely muscled below his coaching staff shorts, she wondered if she'd been lying to herself. Maybe this is exactly what she'd hoped would happen when she told herself she was through waiting in the car for her son.

Stop it, Rosalie. This is Bryce. Fifteen years have passed and in that time too much history to even think of going back.

"Hello, Bryce," she said. "I've come to pick up Danny. I thought he'd be in your office."

Bryce opened the door and stepped in. "He's still out on the field."

Rosalie followed him in the door. "Oh?"

"Yeah. I just came in to get a stopwatch. We're timing Danny in some sprint drills."

"We? Who else is here?"

"A guy named Gordon Capps."

Rosalie knew the name. "Doesn't he own that sports bar and grill over in Donaldson?"

Bryce nodded. "Bought the place a couple years ago after he retired from coaching professional football."

"He used to play for the Falcons."

"That's right. He's helping me out this year with the Wildcats."

Rosalie resisted saying that a volunteer with Capps's credentials was pretty impressive. "What's he doing with Danny?"

Bryce leaned his hip against his desk. "Cappy is our offensive coordinator. Who better to evaluate a potential quarterback?"

Rosalie narrowed her eyes. Danny was being evaluated? "Wait a minute," she said. "I told Danny he could come in and talk to you. That's all. I didn't know he'd try out for a position today."

Bryce looked down at the floor, rubbed his index finger over his chin. "Wow. This is a bit awkward." But when he immediately returned his attention to her, there didn't seem to be any doubt in his eyes. "Danny told me you were behind his decision. And to tell you the truth, I kind of wondered what had made you do the one-eighty."

She wanted to be angry with Bryce, but knew that reaction was irrational. This was all Danny's doing. "My son obviously interpreted our conversation to suit his own purpose. And this explains why he wasn't outside when he was supposed to be. I've been in the parking lot for thirty minutes." She brushed an errant strand of hair off her forehead and felt an inexplicable need to justify her appearance. "I just came from the gym."

Bryce gave her a slanted smile. "Yeah, I figured."

"Well. I guess I'll go get him." She started to walk to the office door.

"Rosalie, wait a minute."

She turned back around.

"Shouldn't we talk about this?"

No. I don't want to. I don't know what I will say if you convince me that Danny should be here. She exhaled and told herself that a cowardly exit would only weaken her position, and said, "I suppose we should."

Bryce motioned to a chair but remained standing. She sat, crossed her legs. Her right foot starting pumping as if it had a mind of its own.

"What exactly are you hoping will come out of this try-out today?" Bryce asked her.

"You know the answer to that. I don't want Danny playing football."

He crossed his arms over his chest. "Let's be honest, okay? You don't want him playing football, or you don't want him playing for me?"

She couldn't tell him that both scenarios were equally bad, so she said, "I don't want him playing football. And I thought that we came to a sort of agreement yesterday."

"I'd keep him off the team?"

"Yes. I hoped."

"To please you?"

"Yes. No!" She was revealing way too much. "Because it's the right thing to do."

Bryce took a moment and then slowly blew out a breath. "We've gotten off to a shaky start since I've been back, Rosalie, and the last thing I want to do is antagonize you further…"

"Then all you have to do is…"

"…but—" he emphasized the word "—I don't agree with you. I don't think lying to your son about his ability and purposely denying him a spot on the team *is* the right thing to do." His gaze seemed to bore into her. "I think it's the entirely wrong thing to do."

He came toward her, settled his hands on the arms of her chair and leaned forward. "He's good, Rosalie. And he wants this."

Her breathing faltered. She almost said the words no mother should utter about her child's desires. She almost said, *But what about what I want?* Bryce was so close she could smell his woodsy aftershave, see the blue of his eyes, smell the sun in his hair. She didn't trust herself to speak so she just looked down.

"Look," he said, still leaning over her. "I know this is hard for you, so I called in Gordon Capps to decide about Danny. I didn't want our past…or our present…to affect Danny's future with the Wildcats. Cappy is an unbiased observer. He won't let our history influence him."

Rosalie looked up and met Bryce's gaze. She wondered if her own eyes held the sadness she saw in his. If Bryce only knew how much history the three of them shared.

"I decided to let Cappy judge Danny's ability, and he has." Bryce stood straight. "He thinks Danny's got real talent. I can't tell the kid he doesn't. It's dishonest, and besides, he would know the truth. Danny knows how he's performed out there today."

Bryce pursed his lips for a few seconds while he seemed to be considering his words very carefully. "Bottom line, Rosalie," he finally said, "if anyone is going to tell Danny he's not on the team, it'll have to be you. If he wasn't honest with you about his plans today, if he wasn't completely truthful with me when he came in here this morning, then you've got a legitimate reason to put your foot down. But that's between parent and child. I'm just the coach, and I'm not going to get in the middle of it."

Between parent and child. Every day lately Rosalie was reminded of the decision she and four others had made fifteen years ago, a decision that excluded her son's father. And every time she heard references to the connection between Bryce and her son, her heart ached a little bit more. The guilt pressed on her shoulders with a greater agonizing weight. How was she ever going to get through football season, the next school year, the rest of her life?

Bryce walked around his desk and took a stopwatch out of a drawer. Then he came to Rosalie and held out his hand. "I do have a suggestion, though. Come outside with me. We'll sit on the bleachers and just watch. Maybe it'll help you understand things more clearly."

She didn't see how, but she stared at his hand,

the strong fingers that had once threaded so perfectly with hers. And almost without thinking, she raised her arm and slipped her hand into his. He pulled her up and walked with her out of the office.

Once in the hallway, Bryce dropped her hand, opened the door and led her to the field. They sat in the bleachers, two rows up. The field was as familiar to her as her own house. She'd watched her brother and Bryce play football on these one hundred yards. She'd attended games here since she'd been teaching at Whistler Creek. Now she stared over the chalk marks and watched her son on the fifty-yard line.

"Hey, Mom!" Danny saw her and sprinted over to the sidelines checking his watch as he ran.

"Hi, there," she said.

"I guess I'm a little late," he admitted.

"It's not the time that's going to get you in trouble," she said. "I'm wondering what part of 'just talk' you didn't understand when we discussed this last night?"

"Well, Mom, you can't blame me for being out on the field today." He pointed to a familiar man who was still as tall and straight as when he had played for the Atlanta Falcons. The man Bryce called Cappy strode toward them. "Look who came to work out with me," Danny said. "It's Gordon Capps."

"Yes, I know who he is."

Mr. Capps stepped up beside Danny. "You got the stopwatch, Coach?" he asked.

Bryce handed the instrument to him and nodded at Rosalie. "Cappy, this is Rosalie Campano, Danny's mother."

Capps gave her a big grin. "You must be awful proud of your boy, Mrs. Campano...."

"It's Rosalie, please," she said.

Cappy settled a hand on Danny's shoulder. "Kid has got some real skills."

Rosalie managed a stiff smile. "I appreciate you saying that, Mr. Capps."

"Call me Cappy. Almost everybody does."

Danny spun a football in his hand. "Hey, Mom, I want to show you something." He looked at Cappy. "Will you center for me, Mr. Capps—just one more time?"

"Sure thing, kid."

They went back onto the field. Cappy lined up a half-dozen footballs and got into a lineman's crouch. Danny stood close behind him. When Cappy snapped up the first ball and delivered it into Danny's hands, Danny stepped back, planted his feet, drew back his arm and let go. The ball sailed thirty yards downfield and landed at the base of an orange cone.

He repeated the drill four more times. Each effort saw the football landing exactly at the base of the intended target. Rosalie watched, experiencing an odd combination of pride and dread. Her eyes blurred when her son arced the ball the last time and spiraled it right where he wanted it to go.

She crossed her legs and layered her hands over her knee. "He's beautiful," she said so softly she didn't think Bryce could hear her.

He leaned close. "Beautiful, Rosie? That seems a strange comment."

She looked at him. "I don't know. Grace, balance, precision. Those characteristics could describe a work of art or my son at this moment." She swallowed, stared straight ahead and whispered hoarsely, "Just like Ricky."

She felt Bryce's hand cover hers. His fingers pressed into her palm and sent a tingle of warmth up her arm. She didn't try to pull away even though she blinked back tears when he repeated, "Just like Ricky."

Danny ran a few sprints before Gordon Capps declared the session officially over. Rosalie and Bryce stepped down off the bleachers and joined them at the sidelines.

"I'd say we've found our backup QB," Gordon said.

Danny was beaming. "Isn't that great, Mom?"

Rosalie didn't trust herself to speak, and when the silence became uncomfortable, Bryce said, "You did great, Danny. But there are still things to consider."

Danny's grin faded. "Like what, Coach?"

"Paperwork," he said. "You need consent forms filled out. You have to have a physical. Our team doctor can do it, or you can use your family physician."

"That's no problem, right, Mom?" His voice rose a notch with barely restrained hope.

"We'll see," Rosalie said.

"And you need to talk this decision over with your family," Bryce added. "Joining the team requires a promise of commitment that affects not just you but everyone in your household."

He looked at Rosalie and she lowered her gaze to the ground. Maybe he was still giving her an out, but she knew now she wasn't going to take it. She couldn't. Crushing her son's enthusiasm was secondary to swallowing her own fears. Danny was going to be a Wildcat football player.

Cappy settled a hand on Danny's shoulder. "I think this calls for a celebration," he said. "Saturday is twenty-five-cent wings night at Cappy's Place. Why don't you all come over and let me treat you? I'll waive the cost of the wings, and we'll watch the Braves game on the big screens."

Danny looked at Rosalie. "That'd be great. Mom, you're not going out, are you?"

"No, but I'd have to see if I'm free to go."

"You can bring your husband, Rosalie," Cappy said. "And anybody else you'd like."

"She's not married," Danny said.

Cappy glanced at Bryce, who remained silent.

"Can I bring my friend Greg?" Danny asked.

"Sure. The more the merrier."

All three males waited for Rosalie's response. After a moment she said, "Right now I don't see a reason we can't be there." She would have to persuade her mother to go with them.

"I'd be glad to pick you up," Bryce said.

"No. Thanks anyway, but I'll drive us. Looks like we may have a small crowd coming." She motioned Danny to follow her. "Let's get going, honey. It's late already."

Bryce walked to the bleachers and picked up a clipboard Cappy had left there. "We'll see you Saturday night then," he said, and concentrated on whatever his assistant coach had written down.

Rosalie and Danny walked around the field house to the parking lot.

"You're being really great about this, Mom," Danny said, climbing into the passenger seat.

On the outside, maybe. She knew her nerves were shot when she had to use two hands to get her key in the ignition. This was happening so fast. Bryce and Danny connected. Football season. Saturday night. Almost as a prayer, she said, "There's still the matter of the physical."

Danny buckled his seat belt. "That won't be a problem. I've passed all the ones for baseball."

He was right. It wouldn't be a problem. She took a deep breath and slowly released it through pursed lips before glancing in her rear-view mirror. The Whistler Creek High School scoreboard soared above the stands, towering above any mere person who stood next to it. That symbol suddenly represented much more than school spirit. It signified that change, big change, was threatening her well-guarded life.

* * *

Late Saturday afternoon, Rosalie and Claudia closed up the stand and headed to the house. Claudia flipped through the paper money she'd stuffed in her pocket from the day's sales. "What should I wear to this shindig tonight?" she asked.

"It's not a shindig, Mom. It's a sports bar, for heaven's sake. You don't need to dress up."

"I wasn't thinking I'd dress up," Claudia said. "In fact, I think this is a good opportunity to wear my jeans."

Rosalie reflected on the trip to the mall six months ago when she'd finally talked her mother into shopping for a pair of real jeans, the kind with a zipper, belt loops, fancy stitching. Previously her mother had bought denim, mostly at Walmart, the stretchy kind of pants with an elastic waist and no ornamentation.

"Everybody wears jeans," Rosalie had said to her mother. "You can wear them for dress up with a nice shirt or go casual with T-shirts."

"I know," Claudia had said. "But when your

father was alive, he liked me to wear skirts for going out. He didn't approve of 'cowgirl attire' as he called it."

Now her mom owned a pair of jeans. Size twelve, stretch denims that fit her perfectly. But she never, ever wore them inside the church, claiming that such an act would make Enzo Campano "turn over in his grave."

"You look great," Rosalie said an hour later when Claudia appeared showered and dressed in the jeans and a peasant-style blouse with a cinched waist. Rosalie herself chose to wear an embroidered tank shirt tucked into a white, knee-length skirt with a flirty ruffle. Not that she was going to flirt with anyone. Far from it.

They set off for Donaldson in Rosalie's car. Claudia sat in the front and Danny and Greg sat in the back. Football was the main topic of conversation. Rosalie remained quiet and concentrated on her driving.

After twelve miles they reached the outskirts of Donaldson, Georgia. The restaurant had multiple neon signs that identified it as Cappy's Place. The building had been a pancake house until celebrity Gordon Capps bought it and renovated to suit South Georgia sports fans. Rosalie hadn't been inside since Gordon took over.

She parked in the gravel lot amid pickups and SUVs. The place looked inviting with cedar siding, a tin roof and a wide veranda across the front. Several patrons occupied outdoor tables, but it seemed most of the customers had opted for air-conditioning on this warm night. Rosalie and her group entered the big double doors and looked for a table.

They needn't have bothered. Gordon Capps came up to them almost immediately. "Hey," he boomed above the jumbled sounds of flat screen televisions and pool table clatter. "Glad you could make it." He led the way to a booth with wide, plush bench seats.

Rosalie sat with her mother. Danny and Greg slid in opposite.

Gordon handed them menus and a remote

control. He pointed to a TV just above their heads. "Pick anything you want to see," he instructed. "Right now the baseball game is on. But if you ladies want some sort of Oprah thing or *The Bachelor* or something, feel free to change the channel."

One look from Danny and Rosalie knew she'd better be content with the game.

She introduced Claudia and Greg to Gordon. The ex-Falcons star patted Greg's shoulder, but his intense green-eyed gaze lingered on Claudia. He offered his hand, she took it, and he held it for several seconds. Claudia's delicate palm looked lost folded in his.

"What'll you folks have to drink?" Gordon asked after a moment.

"Oh, dear," Claudia said. "I think I might just have to order a glass of wine." She practically batted her eyelashes at Gordon. "What do you suggest, Mr. Capps?"

He chuckled. "I'm not sure I know any Mr. Capps around here. It's Cappy or Gordon."

"Fine, then, Gordon, have you a house wine?"

"For you, Claudia, I would recommend our sangria. It's light and fruity. I think you'll like it."

Claudia was happy with the suggestion. Rosalie ordered a Coors Light, the only drink she intended to have, and the boys ordered sodas. Gordon returned with the drinks in under two minutes. On top of Claudia's wineglass someone, Rosalie suspected Gordon, had floated luscious raspberries, strawberries and orange slices, producing quite an elegant drink for only three dollars and ninety-nine cents. Claudia praised the drink as if it had been the offering of a god.

Gordon took out an order pad. "Have you decided on your dinner? Choose whatever you like. It's on the house."

"That isn't necessary," Rosalie said. "We…"

"I invited you, remember," Gordon said. "You're my guests."

"Do you ordinarily wait tables yourself?" Rosalie asked, noting the more-than-adequate number of cute waitresses in abbreviated sports uniforms that Greg and Danny had been ogling.

"No, ma'am, I don't," he said, smiling at Claudia. "But this is a special case."

"Well, thank you, Gordon," Claudia said, returning his grin.

He left to put in the order and Rosalie sipped her beer and pretended to have an interest in the ball game. Until, out of the corner of her eye, she saw Bryce approaching. She took a substantial gulp.

"You're here," he said, placing his hands flat on their table. "You look great, Mrs. C." Then he stuck out his hand toward Danny's friend. "And you must be Greg.

"I saw you come in," he said to Rosalie. "I'm in the middle of a pool challenge, but as soon as it's finished I'll come over."

And do what? Rosalie thought. "We don't want to intrude on your evening, Bryce," she said. "Besides we won't be staying long."

He grinned at her. "Why not? It's Saturday night."

"We have church in the morning," she said. "And then we have to set up the fruit stand. Sunday is a big day."

Bryce looked at his watch. "It's not even eight o'clock, Rosalie. It's not pumpkin and glass slipper time yet."

His friends, Whistler Creek guys Rosalie recognized, called his name and he waved. "Hang around, Rosalie," he said. "I'll be through in a half hour or so."

A half hour. Plenty of time to gobble a few wings and head for home. Bryce left and Gordon brought a huge basket of wings, fresh celery and French fries.

Forty-five minutes later, the pool game was still going strong, and the baskets were empty. Gordon had been a conscientious waiter bringing Claudia another glass of wine and refilling soda glasses. Rosalie figured she'd given Bryce plenty of time to return to their table. She argued mildly with Gordon about the check and gave up when he insisted on treating them.

"Can we play a video game?" Danny asked when she'd strapped her purse to her shoulder.

"No. We should go."

"I'm not finished with my wine, Rosalie," Claudia said.

"Okay. I've got to go the ladies' room anyway. Boys, one game. Mom, drink up. I'll be back in a few minutes."

She walked into the restroom, took her time using the facilities and fluffing her hair for no reason and walked out. She'd only taken one step toward the dining room when someone grabbed her elbow in the darkened hallway, whisked her around and forced her out the back door.

Chapter Eight

Before he had allowed his daughter to date boys, Enzo Campano had taught her a few basic fundamentals of self-defense. She used one of them now as she wrapped her purse strap around her wrist, pulled back her arm, and aimed for her attacker's head.

"Whoa! Rosie, what are you doing?"

Recognizing the voice, she blinked in the scant light from one dim, bare bulb by the back door. Her purse sliced the air about six inches above the head of the man who had crouched down in front of her. "Bryce! Are you crazy?"

He looked up at her, his eyes wide. "Am I crazy? You're the one who just tried to decapitate me."

She yanked up her purse to her shoulder again. "Lucky for you that you have good reflexes or your head really could be rolling across this deck right now."

He stood, arched his back. "I believe it."

"Why did you drag me out here like some caveman?" she asked.

"I didn't drag…" He exhaled, apparently deciding his defense was not going to work with her. "To talk. That's all. Every time I try to get you to hold still for a few minutes, you give me some nonsense about being out of time, having to be somewhere. I'd just like a chance to talk to you without always being on the clock."

She stared up at the bulb, which was hardly visible thanks to a myriad of flying insects seeking its light in the dark exterior of Cappy's. She rubbed her bare arms. "I don't want to talk out here. It's unlit, and we'll get eaten up by mosquitoes."

"No, we won't." He gestured to a large fan in the back wall. "The restaurant exhaust is blowing. The mosquitoes won't light on anything. Besides..." He turned her toward the railing of the narrow back deck, which stood on stilts over a particularly wide stretch of Whistler Creek. "Look across the water. It's actually nice out here."

She did. Hundreds of tiny glowing dots blinked on and off in the forested area. "Pretty," she said. "It's like a convention of fireflies over there."

"Many more than you ever see in town," he said.

She noticed a couple bottles in his hand. "You drinking for two tonight?"

Setting the beverages on the rail, he wiped his palm on his jeans. "One is for you. They're both partly empty now since I sloshed about half on my hand and the deck when you attacked me."

She'd told herself she wasn't going to have more than one beer, but this situation called for an artificial mellower. Since she felt absolutely no effect from the first drink, six wings and a ton of fries ago, she picked up a bottle and took a swig. "Thanks." Dangling her hands over the railing, she said, "What did you want to talk to me about?"

The corner of his mouth quirked up. "The most obvious subject is Cappy."

"What about him?"

"Haven't you noticed that he's hitting on your mother?"

She smiled. "Yeah. But I don't know who's hitting the hardest. Mom is definitely flirting back."

"Imagine that." Bryce took a drink. "Claudia batting those gorgeous Campano eyelashes."

If Bryce was trying for flattery, Rosalie didn't bite.

"I've noticed a change in her," Bryce said. "She looks, well, I don't know how to describe it. Her hair is different for one thing. It's nice."

A memory of a morning almost two years ago flashed in Rosalie's mind. Enzo had been dead two months, and one day, Claudia got up, grabbed her purse and declared she was going to the beauty shop, a trip she normally made only about twice a year to trim her nearly waist-length hair. Rosalie's father liked her hair long, and Claudia had kept it that way to please him.

She returned two hours later with no traces of gray and her hair shorn to loose, curly tendrils framing her face. In one hand she carried a brand new blow-dryer. In the other she had a tube of styling gel the beautician had recommended. That afternoon she and Rosalie had gone into the backyard with a trash can and the bag of giant Velcro curlers Claudia had used for years. They'd spent thirty minutes tossing the curlers at the can and keeping score. Claudia hadn't rolled her hair since.

"She looks like a modern version of that really sexy Italian actress from a few years back," Bryce said. "Gina something."

"Lollobrigida?" Rosalie offered.

"Yeah. Her."

She pretended offense. "That's my mom you're talking about."

"I just mean she looks great. What made her cut her hair?"

Rosalie understood exactly why her mother had taken this step. But she shortened the explanation for Bryce. "Life changes affect different people in different ways," she said. "In Mom's case I think she combated her grief over losing Dad by deciding she could be a version of herself that she'd always kept hidden for Papa's sake. She needed to redefine herself in a way that would allow her some emotional freedom."

Bryce nodded. "So, does she date?"

"Oh, no. Never. She stays busy with the fruit stand, her church and her friends. And she goes to the beauty shop every five or six weeks now."

"But maybe she'll go out with Cappy?"

Rosalie shrugged. "I kind of doubt it, but you never know."

Bryce toyed with the label on his beer bottle.

"I heard you were counseling people about grief," he said.

"Children and teens, yes."

"That's a good thing to do."

"Well, grieving can be a lonely time in a person's life. It helps to know someone is willing to listen." She paused before adding, "Plus, I'm familiar with the emotions myself."

He took another drink, looked out over the creek. "Sure. I know."

She wasn't going to discuss Ricky with Bryce again, so she picked up her bottle and said, "I've got to go back inside. Mom and the boys are probably ready to go."

"They weren't when I..." He grinned. "...*dragged* you out here. Cappy was sitting with Claudia, and the kids were playing video games."

"Still, if there's nothing else on your mind..."

"There is."

"Oh?"

"Yeah. I was thinking that maybe...well, actually hoping that since your son and I are going to be working together, I thought you might tell me something about his father."

Rosalie's stomach muscles clenched. She gulped back a surge of nausea and attempted to keep her voice calm as she instinctively went on the offensive. "Why do you feel you need to know anything about Danny's father?"

"I've coached lots of boys, Rosalie, from high school to college, and one thing I've learned is that the dads often show up on the field. Some of them just observe. Some of them think they know more about coaching than I do and don't hesitate to tell me so. It's only natural that I would wonder about Danny's father someday showing up."

She gripped the bottle until her knuckles hurt. "He won't."

"How can you be so sure? Isn't he in Danny's life at least to a small extent?"

"No, he's not." The less said the better, even though she was spouting one lie after another.

"Okay. Maybe that's true, but you can't blame me for being curious. Once, just before you hooked up with this guy, you and I were close. Really close. I think it's understandable that I would want to know about the guy who picked up where you and I left off."

Good. His comment made her offensive strategy work. "So this is about me, not Danny?"

He thought a moment. "Both, I guess."

She took a drink, set her bottle on the railing and flexed her stiff fingers. "He doesn't concern you, Bryce." She glanced at the starlit sky half expecting a bolt of lightning to crack the deck in two between her feet.

"How can you say that?"

The steel edge of Bryce's voice made her look at him.

"I tried contacting you repeatedly," he said. "You ignored all my calls and letters. And you took up with someone else within a few weeks of my leaving. And I use the term 'took up' loosely."

She bit back an angry response. What he just said was exactly what she wanted him to believe, even if her reputation suffered, so she kept quiet.

"I know you, Rosalie. You don't give yourself easily. This guy had to have been special."

"He wasn't special," she said, fighting the burning in her eyes. "I was hurting. I'd just lost both you and Ricky."

"You didn't lose me, Rosie. You pushed me away."

She looked into his eyes and knew she couldn't defend what was absolutely true. "Okay, maybe I did. But I felt so alone, and I made a mistake with Danny's father. That's all there is to it. I made a decision to raise Danny in my home with Mom and Poppa. I've never once regretted that choice."

His eyes crinkled in thought. After a moment he said, "Wait a minute, Rosie. Does Danny's father even know you got pregnant?"

She rubbed her fingertips over her eyelids willing her brain to send a response to her lips.

"Rosie?"

She breathed out the air she'd been holding

in her lungs and looked at him. "You're venturing into territory you have no right to explore, Bryce. This is my history. I dealt with it the best way I knew how. I don't owe you any explanation for what I did."

She closed her eyes again and flattened her hand over her pounding heart. She was the worst sort of sinner. One who justified every wrongdoing with the best intentions.

He touched her arm. Her eyes jerked open. "Do you ever think about us, Rosie? About those weeks at the beginning of summer?"

Only every time I look in my son's blue eyes, pick up a yearbook, go to Benton's, see a picture of Ricky... She pushed those thoughts away and said, "I've learned not to dwell on the past."

"Lucky for you," he said. "I haven't learned that lesson yet."

"What are you talking about? You've been married. You obviously moved on just like I did."

He seemed to concentrate on his index fingers tapping together. "I moved on because that seemed like what I should do." He returned his gaze to her. "That's not to say I didn't love my wife. I did. But I ignored the signs that underneath all the...well...emotional stuff that happens, we weren't exactly made for each other."

"What do you mean?"

"We had different goals. I wanted kids. She didn't."

Rosalie took another drink and found it hard to swallow.

"She counted on two good incomes supporting our household and didn't think my coaching salary qualified. Ultimately she wanted a career and big-city life. I wanted South Georgia." He stared beyond the creek. "Now that I'm back, I know coming here was the right decision, even if my failed marriage was collateral damage."

"Where is your ex-wife now?"

"She lives in Maryland and works in broadcast journalism. She's involved with a guy twenty years older than she is who has grown children. Everything has worked out as it should."

"Even for you."

A sound between a chuckle and a snicker came from his lips. "Not quite."

"No?"

"There's still the matter of you."

"Me?" Rosalie's cheeks flushed. She wrapped her hands around the bottle hoping the cool glass would combat a rapidly escalating internal thermometer. Looking away from him was impossible. He held her gaze with a concentrated stare. "I don't see how I play into your future, Bryce."

He half smiled. "Oh, come on, Rosie. You're a factor in my past, my present, and now, since I'm back, since Danny is on the team…since I've seen you again, you're going to play a part in my future."

"Not in any significant way," she said. "Football is between you and Danny."

He frowned. "That's bull and you know it.

I'm aware every day of how you feel about Danny being on the team."

"I've accepted Danny's decision."

He smirked. "Right." He lightly tapped her chest. "In here, you're hoping he changes his mind."

That was true, but Rosalie knew he wouldn't.

"Besides," Bryce said, "I'm not just talking about football."

Tingles of alarm rippled through Rosalie's body. She sensed this conversation was about to become intimate. This man, who was once the most important person in her life, was about to say something that could melt her resolve, turn her legs to mush, test her heart and bring back all the pain from the past. She took a quick swallow of beer and set the bottle back on the railing. "I've got to go."

He wrapped his hand around her arm. "Not yet."

"Bryce…"

"Don't you understand, Rosie? We're not finished. We never were. I want to go back to the way it was. I want to go forward to see what it could be like. I want to know if there could be an *us*."

His hand seemed to scorch her arm where he gripped her. She needed to escape. Part of her wanted to stay and see if his touch could warm her to the core like it once did. But since she knew the answer already, that was a bad idea. "Fifteen years have passed, Bryce," she said. "That's too much time, too much history."

"I don't believe that."

"Then it's the beer talking. You and I are victims of a past that wounded us more than we can ever…"

He moved his hand to her chin, stopping her from speaking. "We're not victims, Rosie. We're alive. We're here. We're feeling something." He lowered his head. "We owe it to ourselves to…"

She shook her head. "No…"

His lips touched hers, gently at first then with more urgency. Her breath caught in her lungs. Her instincts warned her to back up, to run.

But crazy emotions, just like the ones from that first time, swirled in her head and made her stay, savor, respond.

His fingers tangled in her hair. She opened her lips and he swept his tongue inside, circling, deepening the kiss. She smelled wild jasmine from the creek, not peaches. She tasted beer, not champagne. But still she knew she would always remember this kiss just as she'd always remembered the first one. And the voice in the back of her mind, the one that had made her cautious every day of her life for the last fifteen years, warned her against allowing any more such guilty pleasures.

She meant to pull her head away, to order him to stop, but the sound that came muffled from her mouth was more a sob. A sound of regret, deep and intense. She put the flat of her hand on the railing, encountered the bottle and heard it sink into the creek with a watery plop.

Bryce lifted his head. A cool breeze fanned her moist lips. He smiled. "I had to do that, Rosie. I had to know."

Her head cleared and with it came the return of the oppressive guilt. "This can't happen again, Bryce."

The smile stayed in place. "I'm hoping you don't mean that. I don't think you do."

"I do mean it. We can't go back."

"Why? Because you'll never forgive me for what happened to Ricky?" His words were strained, as if he truly feared her answer.

She couldn't hurt him. She would never forget the day that Ricky died, the way he died, but she had forgiven Bryce. "No, it's not that."

"Then what?"

I'll never forgive myself. She shook her head. "I've got to go." She blinked, looked over the railing. "The beer bottle. We can't leave it there. The creek is our best natural resource…" *For God's sake, stop talking, Rosalie!*

"I'll get it," he said. He touched her cheek. "Everything will be okay."

Did he understand? Did he sense her inner turmoil? Did he see her for what she truly was? She nodded once and fled into the restaurant.

Chapter Nine

The minute she got in the car, Rosalie turned on the radio. She kept the volume at a moderate level, high enough to keep from having to carry on a conversation with her mother and the boys, and low enough to hear herself think. She pulled out of Cappy's parking lot onto the highway, and her mind was immediately bombarded with noisy, not-to-be-ignored thoughts pinging inside her head like hailstones on the trunk of a car.

First of all, she couldn't take back the kiss. It had happened. She still felt Bryce's lips on hers—warm and hungry, as perfect as she had remembered. So what was she supposed to do? Let him kiss her again as she knew he wanted to? As, God help her, she wanted him to? That would be a crazy, reckless path to take. Because as certainly as she couldn't take back a kiss, she couldn't change the past.

Her eyes stayed glued on the white stripes rushing by her tires as she sped along the two-lane road. But the eyes in her mind took her to a different place, a time almost sixteen years ago. As if it had happened only yesterday, she was in Marjorie Benton's kitchen as the sun set. Five people sat around the heavy pine table. Five people who would decide the future without the one person whose opinion mattered that night. Bryce had left two weeks before and was living in a dormitory at the University of Texas.

Her father had called the Bentons and said that he, his wife and daughter were coming over. That was the plan he'd set that morning when he had learned that Rosalie was pregnant. He'd taken the day to think over his decision. After all, the family had just lost their other child. Enzo Campano had to think rationally, without emotion, so he would do the right thing. Facing the Bentons, he'd ultimately concluded after dinner, was the right thing.

Once brief pleasantries were exchanged and Marjorie Benton offered coffee, which was refused, Enzo was the first to speak. "Roland, you and I have known each other many years. I have always given you a fair day's work for a fair day's pay. I respect you."

Bryce's father nodded. "The respect is mutual, Enzo."

"Then I'll come right out and say it." First looking at his wife and daughter, Enzo turned to Roland and said, "Rosalie is going to have a baby. The father is your son."

Marjorie Benton gasped, covered her mouth with her hand. Roland pinched his lips together and stared down at his clasped hands for one of the longest minutes of Rosalie's life. Then he looked at her. "You're sure?"

"Yes, sir."

"But how can you know for certain that it's Bryce's?" Marjorie objected. "Why would you assume…"

"Marjorie!" Roland's sharp warning silenced her.

Rosalie bowed her head.

Roland addressed his next question to Enzo. "Have you made a decision about what you want to do?"

"We believe in the sanctity of life," Enzo said. He gently patted Rosalie's hand. "My daughter will have the baby. No other option is conceivable to us."

Even tonight, driving on this dark road, Rosalie could clearly envision her father's strong hand over hers in the bright light of the Bentons' kitchen. She still saw the dusting of dark hair on his work-thickened knuckles, the shadows of Benton earth under his fingernails. In that moment she had found her strength from the hand that had packed bushels of produce as earnestly as it had held a Bible in church. Enzo had spoken for all of them. No other option was conceivable.

Marjorie made a sound like a sob, and everyone at the table looked at her. "Are you going to give the baby up for adoption?" she asked, her tone almost hopeful.

"No, ma'am," Rosalie said.

"Then what are you asking of us?" She paused as a look of fear etched her face. "Have you told Bryce?"

Rosalie shook her head.

Roland slid back his chair and started to stand. "I will call him to come home."

"No!" Rosalie's voice was firm.

"You want to call him yourself? I understand."

"No, sir."

Roland settled back in his chair. "I know you and Bryce had feelings for each other before… well, before your family's tragedy. Anyone could tell. Bryce will do the right thing by you, Rosalie."

Enzo cleared his throat. "By the right thing, you mean marriage?"

Marjorie muffled another sob.

"Of course," Roland said. He gave his wife a stern look. "We will be happy to welcome Rosalie into our family."

"You think as I do, Roland," Enzo said. "I immediately saw marriage as the only solution. It is what we would have done in the old country."

"Then we must tell Bryce as soon as possible."

Rosalie couldn't bear to look into her father's sad eyes. Her decision had disappointed him, but she couldn't think about that now. She stared at her mother and waited for Claudia's slight nod of encouragement. The time had come to tell the Bentons that she would not, could not, marry their son. Everything had changed, especially her fantasy of being in love with Bryce. "Mr. Benton," she said. "I don't want to get married."

Marjorie's sigh of relief echoed in the large room. Roland pretended not to hear.

Enzo raised his hands in a sort of supplication. "You see what I am up against here. This is why we've come over tonight. I thought you might help me persuade my daughter that marriage is the proper course."

Roland leaned toward Rosalie. "Don't you want your baby to have a father?" he asked.

Rosalie cleared her throat. "I don't want him to have a father who might always resent what he gave up to stand by me. Bryce left Whistler Creek to make something of his life. Why should he sacrifice everything he's worked for because of what happened one night?"

"Because what happened that night resulted in a baby," Roland said. "Bryce's baby."

"The baby will be fine." Rosalie looked at her mother who had remained silent but now gave her a smile. "My mother and I have talked this over. I will raise the child in our home. My father will be there to guide him."

"I am willing to do that, Rosie, of course," Enzo said, "but it's not the same thing."

"My baby couldn't ask for a better father than you, Poppa."

"I can't disagree," Roland said. "Enzo, you are a fine man. But what about your own future, Rosalie? What will you be giving up to raise this baby?"

Rosalie had thought through all this. And her dreams of going to college had already been put on hold once. So they would be again.

"Yes, Rosalie," Marjorie said. "If you raise the child here in Whistler Creek people will talk. What if your reputation suffers? What if you can't find a job to support the baby?"

"I'm not worried about that," Rosalie said. "People might talk at first, but they will find other matters more important than me and my baby. This is my home. I want to raise my son or daughter here."

Marjorie's eyes widened in shock. "But everyone will know."

"They will know that I had a baby," Rosalie

said. "No one will ever know who the father is. Outside of this room anyway. I will never tell that the father is Bryce."

"But that's just it," Roland said. "Bryce should know. This is his child we're talking about."

"I think Rosalie is doing the right thing," Marjorie said.

Roland gave her a hard stare as the room settled into a drawn-out silence.

Finally Rosalie said, "I don't want Bryce to know because I don't want to marry him, Mr. Benton. I don't want to marry your son. And if I won't marry him, why should his life be interrupted?" She thought about saying more, stating her case even more emphatically. She could tell him that the image of that horrible day in the park would stay with her forever, that she could never get back the feelings she once had for Bryce. But she suspected he already knew that.

He drummed his fingers on the table before

focusing on Rosalie again. "I want to abide by your wishes, Rosalie," he said. "Yet…"

"Those are my wishes, sir. I won't change my mind."

"I still think Bryce should be a part of making decisions about the baby's future, your future."

"Bryce is gone," Rosalie said. "His own future is laid out before him almost like a road map, Mr. Benton. College football, perhaps the pros. Think what he will be giving up if he hears this news and decides to come home. Do you want to be responsible for ruining your son's life?"

Mr. Benton closed his eyes and pinched the bridge of his nose.

"I don't see why Bryce should give up everything he has worked for when I am willing to assume this responsibility, especially since the baby will have a good and loving home."

Marjorie put her hand on her husband's arm. "Listen to her, Roland. Rosalie makes sense."

Roland dropped his gaze to the tabletop, released a long breath and rubbed the back of his neck. After a minute he said, "I don't like this, Rosalie. It's dishonest."

She stared at him until he looked up, his eyes sad. "Isn't it also dishonest for two people to marry when they do not love each other?" she asked. "Let Bryce live his life. I don't want him involved in mine. I ask you to respect my wishes, my privacy. I wouldn't have even come here tonight if Poppa hadn't insisted. Please, sir, this is best."

He didn't speak for more than a minute. But finally said, "What about you, Rosalie? It's not fair that you should give up your dreams if Bryce sacrifices nothing."

"It's all right, Mr. Benton. Since Ricky…well, my dreams don't seem as important anymore." She placed her hand over her stomach. "Now I have a new dream, and it's okay."

Roland smiled. "I understand, but still, I remember Bryce telling me that you want to go to college. Is that still true?"

"I wanted to be a teacher," Rosalie said. "And maybe someday…"

Roland looked at his wife. Marjorie's attention was guarded as she waited for what he might say.

"Let us help you," he said after a moment. "I insist on supporting you through the pregnancy and beyond until you are able to financially care for the child."

"That is not necessary," Enzo said. "I will take care of my family."

"I know you would, Enzo, but this is what Bryce would do if he were involved. It's only right." He waited for his wife to agree, and after a moment she shrugged one shoulder in acceptance.

"And you will go to college, Rosalie," Roland said. "I will pay your tuition and board. You can get your teaching degree, and then we will reevaluate your situation."

Rosalie forced herself to swallow. "What? You would do that?"

"We would consider it an honor."

A spark of pure joy ignited inside Rosalie. Possibilities swam in her mind's eye where, in the last weeks, only grief and sadness had consumed her. This is what she'd always wanted. Could she allow herself to hope that this baby, this unexpected result of loving Bryce, might actually help her to attain her dream? Would her father allow such generosity?

Enzo cleared his throat. "I cannot accept your charity."

Rosalie's heart sank to her stomach. The little her family had saved for Ricky's expenses would never cover her board and tuition.

"It's not charity, Enzo," Roland said. "It's a gift to the daughter of a longtime employee. It's an investment in the future of my grandchild, as well. I want to do this. Even if I can't acknowledge this baby as a member of my family, at least give me the peace of mind of knowing I helped make his entrance into the world a little easier for his mother."

"Please, Poppa," Rosalie said.

Finally Claudia spoke, but she kept her voice low as if she wanted her family to be the only ones to hear her. "I think this is a wonderful plan, Enzo. Rosalie can go away for her first year of school, have the baby and come home to finish out at the extension branch. I will follow when she needs me, and when she returns to us, the baby will already be a part of her life and not an object of speculation for nine months."

Everyone in the room waited, silent, eyes focused on Enzo. When Rosalie thought she might crawl out of her own skin, he looked at her and said, "If this is what you want…"

She hugged him. Claudia squeezed his hand. Roland smiled tentatively. He obviously still had doubts.

And Marjorie reminded them all of the cost. "I urge you to remember your promise, Rosalie," she said. "Bryce will not be told."

As Rosalie pulled up in front of Greg's house, the consequences of the promise she had made that night were startlingly clear. It had been easier to make the promise then than it would be to keep it now.

* * *

Two days later at 8:00 a.m. on Monday, Rosalie came into the kitchen and took two mugs from the cupboard. After setting the cups on the counter, she opened the pantry to get coffee.

Wearing her chenille bathrobe and fuzzy slippers, Claudia breezed into the room, gently nudged Rosalie out of the way and reached for the coffee container.

"I was doing that," Rosalie said.

Claudia lifted the plastic lid. "You never make the coffee strong enough. I'll do it."

"Fine." Rosalie took bread from the wooden box next to the sink and set plates on the table.

"I heard you come in last night," Claudia said as she scooped granules from the extra-large tin. "My light was still on. Why didn't you come in to tell me how your date with Ted was?"

"There wasn't anything to tell."

"Didn't you go to a movie?"

"Yes."

"What did you see?"

Rosalie thought a moment. "I don't remember the name. It was Tom Cruise in some action, intrigue thing. A guy movie."

"Didn't you go out afterward?"

"No. I had a headache."

Claudia dumped grounds into the Mr. Coffee. "Really? You don't usually get headaches."

Yeah. Except for the last ten days. "And your point is?" she said.

"No point. I'm just wondering if you and Ted are cooling off."

Rosalie put two slices of bread in the toaster and depressed the button with more force than was necessary. "We had never heated up, Mom. We're just friends."

"I'm not so sure Ted views your relationship that way."

"How would you know that?"

"Don't you ever kiss or anything?"

Of course they kissed. They kissed last night. Only Rosalie hadn't felt a thing. Not like the night before…

She reached in the refrigerator for the butter

and jelly. When she set the items on the table, she noticed her mother was still staring at her. "Is there a reason for this inquisition?" she asked.

A decidedly smug expression lingered on her mother's face. "What is it about Ted that you don't like, Rosie?" Claudia asked. "Is it that he has two children?"

Rosalie dumped cereal into a bowl, spilling honey nut circles on the countertop. "How can you even suggest that, Mom? I love children. I have one, you know. Plus I'm a teacher, for heaven's sake. I counsel children at the Brighter Day Center."

"Then it must be something about Ted's personality."

Rosalie banged the bowl on the table. "There's nothing wrong with Ted, Mother. He's fine. He's nice. He's absolutely swell." She set milk on the table. "But, if it's okay with you, I've decided to stop seeing him socially."

Claudia stared at the constant dribble of liquid going into the coffeepot as if she were watching molten gold. "Oh, it's fine with me. I'm the last one to interfere in your life, Rosie."

Rosalie sighed. "Ted deserves someone who really cares about him. That's all. I've been stringing him along, and I don't want to do that. I really don't see any future for us."

Her mother fiddled with the pot handle as if that would speed up the brewing process. "Not since Bryce came home, anyway," she mumbled.

"What did you say?"

"Nothing." She slid over the mugs to the pot. "You should butter the toast. Coffee's ready."

Rosalie frowned. "Make mine a double."

Claudia ignored the smart remark, placed the cups on the table and sat down. She stirred her coffee until Rosalie brought the plate of toast. "You don't have to rush off right away, do you?" she asked when Rosalie had taken the seat across from her.

"No. I'm starting on lesson plans this morning so I'll be in my room for the next few hours.

This year I'm determined to have at least the first month of plans ready when school starts."

"Sounds like a good idea."

Rosalie took a sip of coffee. "Why do you ask?"

"Because there is something I wanted to talk to you about."

Obviously, Rosalie thought. Apparently they weren't through dissecting the recent events of her life. She sighed. "Okay, but if this is about Ted…or anyone else…"

Claudia smiled. "It's about me actually."

"Oh. Well, all right. Go ahead."

Claudia spread jelly on her toast. "You know I loved your father with my whole heart," she said.

"Of course, Mom."

"I never once looked at another man. I never even *thought* about looking at another man."

Rosalie paused a spoonful of cereal near her mouth and gave her mother an earnest stare. "I never thought you did. You and Poppa were perfect for each other."

"As perfect as any couple can be," she said. "It's been two years since Enzo left us."

"I know. So what is this about?"

"I had a phone call last night," Claudia said. "It came as quite a surprise." When Rosalie didn't respond, she added, "It was from that man who owns the restaurant in Donaldson."

"Gordon Capps?"

"Yes, him."

Rosalie set the spoon back in the bowl. "What did he want?"

"He asked me out. Can you imagine? A man asking me on a date?"

Actually, Rosalie couldn't imagine such a scenario. But she wasn't about to admit that. "Sure, Mom. You're an attractive woman."

"He was quite chivalrous considering…well, considering we hardly know each other."

"What did he say?"

"He said he hoped I didn't mind that he'd gotten our home phone number. I naturally said that we're listed in the book, so I didn't mind at all."

Rosalie could guess where Cappy had gotten the number. "And then he asked you out?"

"Yes. He asked me to dinner for Wednesday night."

"And what did you say?"

"I was shocked, of course. The invitation was unexpected, out of the blue, really. I didn't have time to think."

"So, again, Mom, what did you say?"

"I said yes."

Rosalie wasn't sure how she felt about this. "And now that you have had time to think, what would you have said?"

"I believe I would have said yes anyway." Claudia took a sip of coffee. "What do you think, Rosie? Is it all right with you?"

She would need some time to sort through the emotions that this admission had awakened in her. Her mother dating? And Gordon Capps was so closely connected to Bryce. But she said, "Sure. It's fine. It's wonderful, in fact."

Claudia grinned. "Really?"

"Really."

"This whole dating thing has me pretty shook

up. I haven't dated since I was nineteen and met your father. Now I'm fifty-four. I'm sure the rules have changed."

Rosalie reached across the table and covered her mother's arm with her hand. "The rules are what you make them, Mom, though I'm hardly an expert on this topic."

"But Gordon is practically a stranger. What will I talk about?"

"Mom, you and Poppa went to supper and the movies every other Saturday night. What did you talk about with him?"

"Oh, we talked about you kids, and football, and people we both knew..."

"One of those is a safe topic," Rosalie teased. "Bone up on field goals and fumbles and penalties. You'll be fine."

"Well, I'm committed now. I won't go back on my promise."

"No. Promises should be kept." *As long as no one gets hurt.*

Claudia sighed. "You know, Rosie, being single again is very confusing. On one hand,

I've had to adjust to thinking for myself, doing for myself. On the other hand, my world has opened up to possibilities I never thought I would be considering. It's exciting and scary all at the same time."

"I'm sure it is, Mom."

"Men," Claudia said as if the weight of the world had suddenly settled on her shoulders. "They can be problematic, I suppose. But they can also be the reason for those possibilities. I feel old and wise for having been married to one. Yet I feel young and inexperienced and, well, *revitalized* for letting one into my life at this stage. It's crazy, isn't it?"

Rosalie smiled, carried her dishes to the sink and thought, *Tell me about it.*

Chapter Ten

Tuesday at noon Bryce pulled into his parents' driveway and got out of his truck. Despite having the AC on full blast driving from the high school, his T-shirt still stuck to his back. Nothing quite like South Georgia heat and humidity, he thought, opening the garage door. But his three-hour session with Cappy and Danny Campano had convinced him of one thing. Danny was no sissy. He'd learned techniques for throwing the ball and listened to basic pattern plays without complaining about the temperature.

Before going in the house, Bryce loaded cartons of his personal belongings from the garage floor into the cargo bed of his truck. One more trip from Little River Road to Fox Hollow and he would have everything moved to the new house. He dusted his hands on his shorts and walked through the mudroom to the cool kitchen. His mother was standing over the sink with her watering can. Bryce wiped his feet and she turned toward him.

"I thought I heard you in the garage," Marjorie said, wrinkling her nose. "You're all sweaty."

"Don't I know it." He opened the refrigerator, reached for a bottle of water and unscrewed the cap.

"Don't sit on any of my good furniture," Marjorie said.

Bryce pulled out a chair at the kitchen table. "Can I sit here if I don't lean back?"

"Okay. You want a sandwich? I'm about to fix one for your father."

"No, thanks. I can't eat until I cool down. Where is Dad?"

"He's at the produce warehouse. I told him not to go in this heat, but you know your father. You'd think after his heart attack he'd be more careful."

Bryce sat. "He'll be okay. The fans work really well in there."

"I've got turkey and cheese."

"No, really, Mom. I'll get drive-through somewhere on my way to my house."

She frowned and watered a plant in her greenhouse window. "Your house. I'll never get used to hearing that. You're still closing on that place tomorrow?"

"I am."

She shook her head and moved on to another plant.

Bryce took a gulp of water and twirled the bottle between his hands. "Mom, can I ask you something?"

"Of course."

"You've got so many connections in this

town, you've always known what's going on, who's doing what, that sort of thing."

"I must admit, people do call me first when news breaks. I don't know why that is, but Marjorie Benton seems to be the source for local gossip."

Bryce smiled. He knew his mom had her own phone tree network which she instituted as soon as she heard anything. Whistler Creek rumors would fly when Marjorie Benton got wind of a good one.

"I want to ask you about Rosalie Campano."

She stopped watering and set the can on the counter. Without turning around she said, "What about Rosalie?"

"I'm working with her son."

She faced him. "You are? Since when? I thought he plays baseball."

"He does, but he came to me last week and expressed interest in football. He tried out and is now officially on the team. Going to play backup quarterback." When his mother didn't comment, Bryce added, "Kid's got real talent. Almost like football is in his blood."

Marjorie wrapped her hands around the edge of the counter. For a moment Bryce thought she might have swayed, but if so, she recovered quickly.

"Well, of course he's got talent, Bryce," she said. "His uncle, Rosalie's brother, played quarterback, didn't he?"

"Yeah. Ricky was great."

She exhaled. "So there you have it."

"Yeah, maybe," Bryce said. "But I'm wondering about Danny's father."

Marjorie picked up the watering can and got back to her chore. "Can't help you there."

"You never met the guy?"

"Why would I meet him?"

"I don't know. You meet nearly everybody who comes into town."

"Maybe he never came here."

"But surely you heard something about him. Whistler Creek is a small town. And when a hometown girl has a baby, I'd think people would talk."

Her back stiffened. She put the can down with a thud and focused on her son. "Bryce, I wrote you about this when it happened. Do I need to fill you in again?"

True, Marjorie had told him that Rosalie had had a baby. But in the last few days, Bryce had felt the need for clarification, fact checking. The baby's conception couldn't have occurred long after Bryce and Rosalie had made love. He needed to be sure. "I'd appreciate it," he said.

Marjorie expelled a long-suffering breath. "Rosalie was grieving back then, as you know."

"Right."

"But apparently once Ricky was…gone, her parents decided she would benefit from going to college. They must have had some money saved up to contribute to Ricky's education. So they used it to send Rosalie to the University of Georgia in Athens."

"And then?"

"Well, she was there a year, a little over a

year actually. I think she came back to town in the middle of that next summer. And when she returned, she had an infant child."

"How old was the baby?" Bryce asked.

Marjorie gave him an exasperated look. "He was an infant, Bryce. Not more than a couple weeks old."

Bryce did a quick calculation as he'd done when he had first heard that Rosalie had had a baby. According to his mother's version of the story, which was the same now as when it happened, Rosalie had the baby almost twelve months after the two of them had been together. "Did she ever talk about the father, her relationship with him?"

"Certainly not to me, Bryce! I've never been close to the Campanos. I would assume she talked to her parents. After all, they agreed to take her and her child into their home. They must have known the details."

Of course Enzo and Claudia took in Rosalie. That was the kind of people they were. "So you never heard anything about who the father was or how Rosalie met him?"

Marjorie sighed. "How many times do I have to tell you, Bryce? I didn't hear anything and I certainly didn't ask. Goodness, it wasn't my business. The people of this town just accepted Rosalie when she came back and continued her education locally. No one made a big deal about the baby. As far as I know, little Danny Campano was just like any other kid growing up here. And Rosalie never suffered any effects from coming home. She was hired at the high school, and she is respected by the community."

Bryce knew that was true. He'd never heard one bad word about Rosalie. She was obviously a caring mother, a good teacher and a contributing member of Whistler Creek. He had to assume that she had met some guy at school during her period of grief, hooked up for a time, and then their relationship had ended.

But her decisions at that time of her life still hurt him. And Bryce would always wonder…

after what they'd shared, how they'd felt about each other, why couldn't she have turned to him? He'd certainly tried to reach her. Why couldn't she have forgiven him when she had needed a shoulder to cry on? His would have been strong enough.

"Roland, what are you doing?"

His mother's cry shook Bryce from his thoughts. He turned to the kitchen door and saw his father carrying a large crate of produce. He immediately took the carton from his dad's hands and set it on the table.

"Thanks, son," Roland said and then looked at his wife. "I'm bringing the things you asked for, Marjorie. Green peppers, corn, peaches, potatoes. You gave me a list this morning."

She studied the crate, ticking off the contents on her fingers. "I didn't mean you should carry them into the house on your own!"

"Yeah, Dad," Bryce said. "The doctor said you shouldn't carry anything heavier than a six pack for the next few weeks."

"I'm not a cripple, Bryce. I can certainly manage a carton of vegetables."

Marjorie stared at her husband before tilting her head at Bryce. "You see what I put up with?" she said.

He grinned. "I'm going up to take a shower. Then I'm heading out to…" He almost said "my house" but thought better of it. No sense antagonizing his mother further. "…to the Harbin place."

"Are you staying here at least tonight?" Marjorie asked.

"Yes, but I'm having a bed delivered out there today, so I'll be moving out permanently tomorrow."

She sighed again, began pulling produce out of the box. "I just don't see why…."

Bryce stopped at the entrance to the dining room. "Mom…"

She waved him off. "Fine. Go take your shower. I'll fix your father a turkey sandwich."

As he climbed the stairs to the second floor, Bryce decided he'd drive extra slow when he passed the Campano place. Maybe Rosalie would be at the produce stand. Maybe she'd been thinking about the kiss as much as he had.

Rosalie gave her customer change and handed her a bag of tomatoes. "Thanks, Betty, I'm sure your stew will be wonderful."

The woman got in her car and drove off. Rosalie sat down in a lawn chair and focused on her best friend. "How long have you been home, Shelby? Weren't you supposed to stay in North Carolina for two weeks?"

Shelby shrugged. "I had a relaxing time, but two whole weeks with the parents is too much. I got up yesterday morning, felt restless, packed and left. Had to promise to come back once more before September though."

"So what did you do for fun?"

"No fun," Shelby said. "Just relaxing and eating. Now I'm looking forward to shopping, going out and partying a little before school starts." She gave Rosalie an earnest stare before reaching over the produce stand and picking up a peach. "I'm not a family person like you are." She took a big bite of the fruit. "So what have you got planned for today, besides running the stand? I want you to go to the mall with me."

"I can't," Rosalie said. "At least not until someone comes home to take my place here."

"Where's Danny?"

"He's working with Greg at the car wash for pocket money."

"Where's Claudia?"

Rosalie knew Shelby would appreciate her answer. "Are you ready to hear some news, Shel?"

"Sure."

"Mom's out shopping for a new outfit. She has a date tomorrow night."

Shelby's mouth dropped open. "What? Claudia the Sainted is going out on a date? With who?"

"You might know him, or at least have heard of him. He's a former Atlanta football player and he owns a bar and grill in Donaldson."

"Gordon Capps," Shelby said.

"That's him."

"Boy, when Claudia decides to dip her feet in the dating pool, she goes right for the deep end."

Rosalie didn't quite get the metaphor. "What are you saying? Capps isn't a good guy?"

"No, he is, I suppose. In fact, I'm really impressed. I've seen Capps a time or two. Thick, wavy gray hair, gorgeous build, that nice, outdoorsy complexion. I just meant that Mama C is starting with the best South Georgia has to offer, at least for the geriatric set."

"Oh. Well, good. I'm glad Mom's going out, but I know I'll worry whether he'll treat her right."

Shelby laughed. "Oh, pooh. Don't forget. She's the mother, not you." She took another bite of peach. "So how did this budding romance come about?"

Rosalie briefly mentioned the trip to Cappy's and added, "Mr. Capps is helping out with the Wildcats football team this year. He knows

Danny, and we ran into him when we went for wings the other night."

"Why would Gordon Capps know Danny?" Shelby asked.

There was no hiding Danny's decision. The entire town would know soon enough. "That's another bit of news. Danny has joined the football team."

Shelby pretended to choke on a section of peach. "You've got to be kidding! You don't want Danny playing football."

"No, I don't," Rosalie said. "But in the last year or so, Danny's been searching for a mind of his own and, a few days ago, he found it."

"Bummer for you," Shelby said.

Rosalie let the obvious comment slide. Shelby didn't have a clue about how bummed she was.

"By the way," Shelby said, "speaking of the best South Georgia has to offer, have you seen much of our new football coach?"

Rosalie blanched. Seen. Heard. Felt. Kissed. "I've seen him around some," she said.

Shelby wiped her bottom lip with her finger and licked the tip. "That can't be easy for you."

Shelby had only been in Whistler Creek for three years. How did she know that seeing Bryce would be difficult for her? Rosalie certainly hadn't confided the most secret and intimate details of her association with Bryce to her friend. "Why would you say that?" she responded.

Shelby gave her a coy smile. "I hate to bring up the past, Rosie, but since you never gave me many facts, I had to find some out on my own."

Rosalie's heartbeat increased to a near roar. "Find out what?"

"Remember the night Coach Benton was introduced to the faculty?"

It was only the night that changed everything in Rosalie's life and reopened the guilt she'd thought she'd finally learned to live with. "Yeah. What about it?"

"Well, you left in such a hurry that we didn't

get a chance to talk much about the good-looking Coach Benton."

"What's there to talk about?"

Shelby stared at her. "Only that he's the one who threw the football the day your brother died."

Oh, wonderful. Just what Rosalie had feared. All the past being dredged up and reinterpreted and analyzed. Shelby knew that Rosalie's brother had died in a freakish sort of accident, but Rosalie had never told her the specifics. She sighed. At least this was Shelby. Once she was satisfied that Rosalie was telling her the truth, she could be counted on to not bring the subject up again. "Who told you?" Rosalie asked.

"Ben Stoddard."

Of course. The math teacher had been at Whistler Creek High for thirty years. He'd taught Rosalie, Ricky and Bryce algebra.

Shelby continued. "I bumped into him as I was walking back to my car that night. He casually mentioned that he wondered how your family would adapt to having Bryce back in town."

Rosalie smirked. "And of course you pressed him for an explanation."

"Of course." She finished her peach and tossed the pit into a trash can. They sat silently for a moment. "You should prepare yourself, Rosalie. People must remember and they will talk."

"I know. I guess I'll just avoid crowds. I don't want to relive that day."

"Sure. At least you don't have to worry about me. I won't talk about it unless you want to."

"Thanks. I appreciate that…."

Shelby interrupted her. "However, I can guarantee you that reminders abound in this small town." She pointed down the road where a black pickup approached. "Isn't that our dear coach's vehicle coming now?"

Rosalie exhaled the breath she'd been holding. There wasn't time to run into the house, and

there wasn't a tree big enough to hide behind.
So she just prayed that Bryce would drive on
by. Except his right blinker was flashing.

Chapter Eleven

Just what he had hoped for. Rosalie was at the Campano produce stand. Sitting beside her on a lawn chair was a blond woman he didn't recognize. Bryce pulled onto the gravel surface and cut his truck engine. At the same time, his heart did an odd jump kick of its own. He'd been thinking about Rosalie since Saturday night, and he wouldn't pretend he wasn't reacting to seeing her today.

He got out of the truck and walked to the stand. "Afternoon, ladies."

The blonde he didn't know leaned forward

and said, "Hi, there." Rosalie, dressed in a white tank top and plaid shorts, nodded without smiling.

Bryce stuck out his hand to the woman. "I don't think we've met."

Rosalie looked at the woman. "Shelby, this is Bryce Benton. Bryce, Shelby Lebeau."

"I was at Canfield's big announcement meeting," Shelby said, shaking his hand. "So I definitely know who you are."

He felt a flush creep up his neck. He wanted to live down that unforgettable event. "That meeting wasn't my finest hour."

Shelby smiled. "Nobody sneaks into Whistler Creek, cowboy. When I moved here three years ago, the assistant principal threw a traditional southern tea party with about a hundred and fifty women. I felt like I was on display in a window at Macy's." She frowned, but not unkindly. "Still do feel that way some days."

"I know what you mean." Bryce turned his attention to Rosalie. "How are you, Rosie?"

"Great." She leaned on the stand. "What can I help you with, Bryce?"

Nothing subtle about Rosalie, he decided. He picked up an empty basket and began filling it with vegetables. "The closing on my house is tomorrow," he said. "I have the key so I'm moving some of my stuff in today." He nodded toward the boxes in back of his truck. "I stopped here because I thought I might as well stock the fridge."

"Your name is Benton," Rosalie said. "Why in the world are you shopping for produce here?"

"Convenience. You're on the way to my house." He reminded himself not to let her see the sack filled with veggies his mother had put in the bed of his truck.

"Fine," Rosalie said. "But I'm charging you retail prices."

He grinned. "I can't even expect a house-warming fruit basket from you, Rosalie?"

"I already gave you a backup quarterback."

She almost smiled. "Some men are never satisfied."

"Some men maybe," he said. "But not me. You definitely satisfy me...most times."

Shelby covered her mouth with her hand.

Rosalie grabbed the shopping basket out of his hand and began ringing up his purchases and putting the selections in a bag. "That's ten dollars and seventy-five cents, Bryce."

He gave her a ten and a one. "Keep the change."

"Thanks, I will. So if that's all..."

"It's not."

"What else do you want?"

"Advice. I was hoping to persuade you to come over to my place and give me some decorating tips."

"You're kidding, right?"

"No. There's some furniture in there now, but, as you might imagine, it's pretty worn. I could use a woman's perspective."

Rosalie swept her hand toward her friend. "What about Shelby? She's our home ec and

family relations teacher. She's much more qualified…."

Shelby shook her head. "No can do, kids. I'm
on my way to the mall in a few minutes."

The home ec teacher had a knowing smile on
her face. Bryce decided he liked her. "Guess
that leaves you, Rosalie. Will you come?"

"I'm watching the stand, Bryce. I can't just
leave."

"Sure you can," Shelby said. "I'll stay until
Claudia gets back. That shouldn't be long."

"But you've never done this. How will you
know prices?"

Shelby held up a chart she pulled from be-
neath the counter. "It's all here, right? Cu-
cumbers, two for a dollar, peaches, a dollar a
pound… I can read, Rosie. Go on. Have fun."

Bryce walked to his car and opened the passenger door. "It's settled then. I'll bring you
back here in a little while."

Rosalie looked at him and back at Shelby. Her
lips moved as if she were trying to come up
with a logical explanation for why she couldn't

go. After a moment she shrugged. "Sure. Why not? I've got my cell phone, Shel. Call me if Mom doesn't get back by the time you want to leave."

"Sure thing."

Bryce set his sack of produce on the floor between his bucket seats, waited for Rosalie to get inside, and shut her door. As he walked around the truck he was smiling. He didn't know why it was so important to him that Rosalie see his house. The degree of her enthusiasm could be measured in single digits. But maybe he could change that.

As soon as they turned off Fox Hollow Road into Bryce's narrow drive, Rosalie noticed subtle differences since she'd been here before. Bryce, or someone anyway, had cleared ground foliage, widening the path to the home that would officially belong to him tomorrow. Also, the weeds that had nearly hidden his front porch had been pulled. The porch itself had to be painted, but Rosalie figured that task would be accomplished soon. Already pride was evident all around this humble farmhouse.

Bryce parked in front of the house and just looked out at his property for a moment.

"You've been doing some work out here," Rosalie said.

"I was pretty confident of the closing date. The Realtor gave me the key, so I knew a head start couldn't hurt. That's what's so great about small towns. People trust each other."

They got out of the truck, and Bryce preceded Rosalie up the short set of steps to unlock the front entrance. He swung the door wide. "After you. And keep in mind, this is going to be a work in progress for a while."

Knowing the house had been empty for more than three years, Rosalie expected cobwebs and inch-thick dust. No cobwebs, but there was dust. Otherwise, the parlor was mostly tidy. Once the rustic pine floor was sanded, it could be polished to a shine. The fieldstone around the fireplace looked like it had only recently been applied. The hearth showed remains of past fires but a broom and dustpan would eliminate the ashes.

Despite her personal pledge to remain indifferent to Bryce's new home, Rosalie was delighted with the furniture. She surveyed the maple-framed sofa, matching chairs and tables. The pieces were solid, heavy, masculine, and somehow, just perfect for Bryce.

"It's all dated, I guess," he said. "That's why I need a new perspective." He went to the sofa and slapped the back cushion. Dust rose, and he exaggerated a cough. "What do you think, Rosalie? Donate all of it and start over?"

"I'd keep every piece," she said.

"You would?"

She walked closer and ran her hand over the wide arm of the sofa. A rich patina showed where elbows had rested on the same spot. "You'll have to change the fabric of course," she said. "And a mild wood cleaner will remove soil from the frames without taking away the character."

"Really? You like these things."

She nodded. "I love everything in this room. Why get rid of anything that's such a part of the history of this house."

"So you'd just replace the cushions?"

"Sure. You might consider a beige or tan leather or an earth tone microfiber." Her mind began churning with possibilities. "You can add color and design with pillows and throws." She went to a window and fingered the long drapes. "These have to go, but you could re-place them with shutters and sill-length cur-tains with distinctive tiebacks."

When his gaze followed her around the room, Rosalie was suddenly aware of the misplaced enthusiasm she was showing for a house that wasn't hers. She swallowed and turned to look at his puzzling smile. "What?" she said.

"You're hired."

"Oh, no…"

"Rosie, say you'll help me. We've got a few weeks until school starts. I'll be having ab-breviated practice sessions so I can spend time here working on projects. If we tackle this to-gether…"

"Bryce, no. It's out of the question." She said the words, but inside her there was a creative soul fighting to be let free. Other than the year she'd lived in a single quad room in a college apartment, she'd never had a home of her own. She'd slept in the same bedroom her entire life. Eaten at her mother's table, sat on her parents' sofa. Not one thing of substance had ever been hers. No space had ever reflected her personality except for her classroom at Whistler Creek High School which she tended to overdecorate every year.

Get a grip, Rosalie, she said to herself. This wasn't her home either. It was madness to even think of putting her personal touches on this house. Still, her mind's eye wouldn't let go. She kept picturing soft colors, warm plaids, subtle outdoorsy prints. Furnishings that would define the Bryce she used to know and love. The man she'd thought would never return to

Whistler Creek but who was standing three feet from her now.

"There's nobody else I'd want to do this, Rosalie."

And nobody who'd like to do it more than me. You have to say no, Rosalie.

"Who knows me better than you in this town?" Bryce said.

No one ever could. But say no, Rosalie.

He gave her a little grin. "You'll keep me from turning this place into a monstrosity, and it might be fun."

It would be fun, if the two of you could get past all the tension. But you really must say no, Rosalie.

He touched her elbow. "What do you say?"

She sighed, and someone's voice, a stranger's, said, "I guess I could give it a try...."

"Great."

"If it doesn't take up too much time."

"It won't. We'll work around your schedule."

He pulled her gently across the room. "Let's have a look at the kitchen. I can't afford a total remodel now, but maybe you'll have a few inexpensive suggestions."

She followed him into a bright, spacious room with lots of natural sunlight. Aside from the out-of-date appliances, all the room needed was a coat of paint and some serious elbow grease. "This is a nice area," she said. "Easy to work in."

He chuckled. "Find a good place for a microwave."

His enthusiasm was infectious. Rosalie experienced feelings like the ones she had remembered from when she and Bryce were inseparable as friends. The possibility of stoking the spark of their childhood relationship was too much to resist. Yes, there were challenges being around him now. They shared a difficult history, and they were certainly no longer children. But she'd loved him once as a friend. And those feelings were as alive as they'd ever been. Despite that kiss on Saturday night, she could keep their relationship casual. She could be his friend again.

"Wait here," he said, breaking into her thoughts. "I'm going out to the truck. I'll be right back."

After he left, she wandered around the cheerful space, opening cupboard doors and little-used drawers. She kept busy, not giving herself time to think about what she'd agreed to. In a moment, Bryce came inside, and she viewed him as she once had. In a Dallas Cowboys T-shirt, loose-fitting gray shorts and sandals, he reminded her of the Bryce of old. The boy who'd been her best friend. Back then she hadn't been able to resist his schemes and plans. She couldn't now. But, she told herself again, they were no longer children.

He set two frosted beers on the counter and opened them. Giving her one, he said, "Let's celebrate. You want to see the outside?"

They went into his expansive backyard where recent cuttings lay in neatly raked piles. "I hired somebody to go over my property with a riding mower so I could see clearly to the tree line. A mower is going to be one of my first purchases." He pointed to a couple rickety lawn chairs. "Along with a set of outdoor furniture so I can actually enjoy this space."

She sat in one of the chairs, inhaling the scent of newly mown grass mingled with something woodsy and spicy, the aftershave she was beginning to associate with Bryce. Or perhaps his shampoo. He'd obviously recently showered, and she was suddenly conscious of the fact that she hadn't. Her skin heated under her tank top and shorts. Her nape prickled under her loose hair. But she was sitting in the shade of a giant oak tree and the breeze was cool. She took a sip of beer and pressed the cold bottle to her cheek.

"Is it too hot out here for you?" he asked.

"No. I'm fine."

They sat in silence for a moment until Bryce said, "I've gotten to know Danny. We had a great practice today, and in between workouts I sat him down and we talked."

"Really? What about?"

"About his goals, his family, how he does in

school. I like to get to know my players on a more personal level. He's a great kid, Rosalie. You've done a good job raising him."

She took a sip of beer and felt the burn the whole way down her throat. "It wasn't just me. Mom and Poppa helped."

"And I can see that. I can see Enzo's determination and work ethic in him, Claudia's quiet wisdom. But it's your vitality—your soul—that really shines through, Rosie. Just like you, he's good and caring and spirited. He's your son, no doubt."

Good and caring? She stared out at the trees. If she dared look at Bryce now would he be able to see into that soul of hers and tell that the qualities he was admiring didn't define her as much as he believed.

"Can I ask you something, Rosalie?" he said.

"Not too personal, I hope."

"It is, a little."

"Bryce, I don't think we should dwell on each other's personal histories, or…"

"Rosalie, come on. Except for the last fifteen

years, your personal history is basically my personal history. I was there when you fell off your bike and broke your wrist. I remember the time we were ten years old and you, Ricky and I stripped down to our drawers and went swimming in Whistler Creek at the old mill." He laughed softly. "My dad threatened to tan my hide if I ever did something like that again with a 'young lady.'

"I picked wildflowers for you when you had your wisdom teeth pulled. And I remember how you looked standing next to Johnny Baxter at senior prom. In that light yellow dress, you were the most beautiful thing I'd ever seen. And I hated Johnny Baxter."

She looked at him. "You didn't. Johnny was a good guy."

"Sure, but I hated him just the same. It wasn't until the next morning when you and I were in the orchard with our contraband champagne that I understood why. I hated Johnny because I loved you."

This conversation was venturing into dangerous territory, but Rosalie couldn't help it. She smiled. "Oh."

"So, let me ask you this one question."

"Okay, but I reserve the right to not answer."

"Fair enough." He turned in his chair and looked squarely at her. "Rosalie, that night— the one time we made love…"

He paused, unknowingly giving her pounding heart time to catch up to her careening thoughts. "Oh, jeez, Bryce."

"No, let me finish. Before…it happened…you had gone to the doctor to get a prescription for birth control pills."

"That's right. I did." *But my mother wouldn't sign her consent and I didn't get them.*

"I'm just curious. What happened when you went off to college? I would assume you'd continue with the pills."

Rosalie took a deep breath and responded with a question meant to buy her time. "Why would you think that?"

He gave her a puzzled look as if the answer should be obvious. "Well, you weren't interested in me anymore. And you were heading away from home. You know, freedom, meeting new people, new ideas and opportunities. I'd just think a girl like you would want to be careful."

Rosalie gave herself a mental kick in the head. She should have been prepared for a question like this. But lately, over the last two weeks, she'd discovered she'd been dangerously unprepared in many areas of her life. She fixed her gaze on the pad of her thumb circling the top of her beer bottle and said, "I thought I was being careful. There are risks, however small, to taking birth control pills, and I didn't intend to become involved with anyone, so I stopped them."

"But you did become involved. And pretty quickly."

"I guess you could see it like that. But the fact remains, I didn't *intend* to."

"What does that even mean, Rosalie?"

She stared at him, hoping a sharp look would silence him. No luck.

"I just don't understand," he said. "From everything I can determine, you had unprotected sex with someone. That just doesn't make sense to me."

She stood, took a couple steps closer to the giant oak tree. Without looking at him, she said, "It doesn't have to make sense to *you,* Bryce. Besides, we've been through all this, you and I."

"No. You gave me some pat answers the other night. Now I just want one honest account of how it happened."

She huffed out an indignant breath, heard the rustle of his chair and sensed his footsteps behind her.

"You're mad at me now," he said.

No. I'm just trying to think. She stared at the ground and said, "You're not going to be happy until I give you all the details, are you?"

"I'd like to hear them, yes. I'd like to know how you could go from what we had to what that other guy, whoever he was, gave you." His hand rested on her shoulder. "For a time, the happiest time of my life, by the way, you were my world, Rosie, until that awful day."

She had to give him something. Her reputation as the girl he'd believed her to be had already suffered. Now Bryce would only form more conclusions, and imagining him thinking the worst of her was harder than telling him another lie. What if he thought she went off to college and became some free-spirited girl with a hearty sexual appetite determined to find anyone who could satisfy her loneliness for one night? Or, almost as bad, what if he thought she went through a period of insanity, her choices not her own, her life in a free fall?

She turned around, folded her arms over her chest. "Okay, you want to know? Here it is." She leaned back against the tree when, all at once, her legs didn't feel capable of holding her upright. "I was in a bad place when I went away."

"I understand that. Still…"

"Don't talk," she snapped at him. "You want my story, let me tell it." *Even if it is all a lie.*

"Sorry."

"When I left for school, I was so grateful for the opportunity to go away, to study, to become a teacher. I never thought I'd ever be given that chance." She studied his facial features for any sign that he knew his parents had enabled her to go to college. His expression was impassive so she went on.

"Being in school gave me the chance to get my mind on other things, and I was determined to work hard. You know I was never the best student. Good grades were always a struggle for me. So I wasn't interested in boys or a social life." She let out a long breath. So far she was telling the truth.

Now the path of the story became rocky. "I certainly didn't expect to meet anyone. But I did. Who he was doesn't matter really. One day he was there, being nice to me. We started out studying together, going on walks, that sort of thing. And one night, well…he had a bottle of something. I don't even remember what. I drank some of it, and things got carried away. I made a mistake. One time. A couple days later I saw him taking walks with someone else."

His eyes narrowed. "And that was it?"

"Yep. Done and over. Do I regret it? I regret my foolishness, my gullibility. But every day I thank God for giving me Danny."

"And this guy…he never knew?"

"He doesn't know to this day." She breathed easier now that she was back on the track of truth.

"And that's the way you want it?"

"That's what is best for everyone," she said.

"You didn't think he would be a good father?"

"Bryce, I made a decision based on more factors than his qualifications as a father."

A mix of emotions crossed Bryce's face. Puzzlement, hurt, perhaps even disbelief, but he remained silent, taking in the details she'd provided. After a moment he wrapped his hands around her upper arms. "Thanks, Rosalie. I'm glad you trusted me enough to tell me."

She closed her eyes so he couldn't see into them. "You're welcome."

After a moment, Bryce whispered, "Did you love him?"

She refocused on his face, so close she could feel his warm breath on her forehead. "Bryce…"

"Did you?"

She gave him the kindest answer, but the biggest lie. "No."

His fingers flexed on her arms. "And what about Coach Ted? Do you love him?"

"For heaven's sake, Bryce…"

He cocked one eyebrow and waited for an answer.

She shrugged her shoulder. "Ted and I are no longer seeing each other."

"Ah. Interesting. That means that nothing is standing between us."

Only a huge lie and a fourteen-year-old boy.

He dropped his gaze from her eyes to her chest. She sucked in a quick breath, feeling her breasts strain against the thin fabric of her tank top.

"Nothing but a few inches." Bryce grinned.

"In a fourth-down situation, a few inches can be a challenge in football, but not so much in a situation like this."

He pressed her against the tree. She felt the bark through her top. And then his hand was in the small of her back and he was pulling her toward him. His thighs trapped her legs and his other hand flattened against the tree trunk just above her head. They were perfectly braced as if they were made for each other, meant to be under this tree on this day.

"I kissed you on Saturday night, Rosie," he said, "and I think you liked it."

There was no use lying about that so she just held her breath.

"And I know one other thing. I'm not going to wait another fifteen years before I kiss you again."

His mouth settled on hers. His lips were soft and warm and inviting. As sweet as a first kiss. But then everything changed and the boy in her mind became a fully grown version of the person she'd loved. His mouth ravaged hers, exploring, igniting a young girl's passion into a woman's need. The sensation of being devoured by that hot, hungry kiss tingled through her body and she answered him with equal passion. It was like coming home and finding a treasure she'd thought she'd lost.

A horn sounded in the distance. Bryce raised his head and then returned for a quick nibble of her bottom lip. "We've got to stop this, honey."

"Of course. You're right. This is…" She hardly recognized her own voice.

"No. I mean someone's here. I think it's the deliveryman from the mattress store."

"Oh."

He circled her waist with his arm and led her toward the house. Before they skirted around the side, he planted a swift kiss on her temple. "I'm having a king-size bed delivered today," he said.

"Oh." She was an English teacher, for Pete's sake. Why did her vocabulary disappear around Bryce?

"That's right. You haven't seen the master

bedroom. Why don't you have a look once the bed's in there. Might inspire some ideas." He grinned. "Decorating ones, of course."

"Of course."

"By the way," he said when they came around the front and encountered the delivery truck, "I'll be sleeping here from tomorrow night on. Just in case you get some ideas in the middle of the night that can't wait."

She already had one, and she was pretty sure he knew what it was. Just as she knew it would be impossible to simply remain friends with Bryce Benton.

Chapter Twelve

Rosalie rushed around the house looking for her purse, her car keys, her cell phone. In thirty minutes, at six o'clock, she was meeting with a group of seven- and eight-year-olds who were having difficulty adjusting to the loss of a loved one. She wanted to be at the center at least fifteen minutes early to set up her project for the kids, which meant she had to leave the house soon.

Setting the box of supplies she'd gathered for the children at the front of the house, she went back to her mother's bedroom door and tapped lightly. She couldn't wait much longer for Claudia to come out. "Mom? Are you ready for your big date?"

The voice that answered her was tentative, a cross between excited and nervous. "As ready as I'll ever be. Don't leave yet, Rosalie. I need your opinion about how I look."

"Well, hurry up. I've got to go in about five minutes."

Rosalie went back to the living room to wait. A few seconds later Claudia came out of the hallway. She stood still for a moment before raising a hand to pat her casually styled hair. "Be honest, Rosalie," she said. "What do you think?" Without waiting for Rosalie to answer, she added, "Cheryl down at the beauty parlor suggested we do my hair more like you younger women do with this shiny stuff on it." She leaned into the mirror over the foyer credenza. "I feel practically naked without a bit of hair spray."

Rosalie looked into the mirror over her mother's shoulder. "Mom, you look absolutely stunning."

"Yeah, you're rockin', Grandma," Danny said, coming out of the kitchen with a submarine sandwich in his hand. "Coach Capps is gonna stroke out."

Claudia's brow furrowed. "Well, goodness, Daniel, I hope not!" She smoothed her palm along the seam of a pastel batik skirt. "What about the outfit? Too hippie-ish?"

"Mom, it's gorgeous," Rosalie said. "Where did you find that skirt?"

"Believe it or not, I went to that boutique place on Center Street. The clerk was young enough to be my granddaughter, but she was very helpful."

Rosalie decided the clerk also had a knack with colors and fabric. To the springlike hues in the skirt, she'd matched a sky-blue silk blouse and a shimmering scarf as a belt. A yellow-and-blue moon charm on a black satin ribbon rested just above a revealing hint of Claudia

Campano's cleavage. Rosalie blinked. *Good God, Mom!*

Claudia stared down at the necklace. "It's too much, isn't it?" she said. "That's why you're looking at me like that."

"No, no, nothing like that." Well, maybe. "You look at least ten years younger in that outfit."

Claudia reexamined her image in the mirror.

"Really," Rosalie said. "You look great."

"Hot," Danny said.

Claudia beamed. "Really?"

Suddenly Rosalie felt at least twenty years older than she had two minutes ago. She was surprised that this new venture of Claudia's made her uncomfortable. Fighting an urge to ask her mother when she would be home, Rosalie swallowed and said, "You've got your cell phone, right?"

"Of course." She tapped her small shoulder bag. "It's right here."

"Where are you going?" Rosalie asked.

"I'm not sure. Somewhere that takes reservations, so I expect the Whistler Inn. Although, even the Whistler shouldn't be crowded on a Wednesday." Claudia primped a bit more and said, "You're not worried are you, Rosalie? I'm a grown woman, you know."

"Oh, sure. No, I'm not…" Rosalie couldn't even finish the sentence. What did she know about Gordon Capps? The fact that he played professional football didn't recommend him as a proper date for her mother. "You know," she said, "maybe I can be a few minutes late to the center. I think I'll stick around until Gordon gets here."

"Don't be silly, dear," Claudia said. "You go on. I'll see you in the morning. Don't wait up. I don't know how late we'll be."

Rosalie looked at Danny, who was grinning with obvious teenage amusement. "It's okay, Mom," he said. "I'll tell Coach Capps to be a gentleman."

There being nothing rational left to say, Rosalie picked up her supplies and went to her car. As she drove to the center, she thought about how her safe, secure world had taken an unexpected spin off its axis. She'd lost control of her son. The one man she'd determined would never get under her skin again was now causing an emotional itch that plagued her day and night. And she was mothering her mother!

And what was she doing about it? She'd spent yesterday afternoon at the Fabric Barn picking out swatches for Bryce!

She pulled into the empty parking lot and got out of her car. At least she was the first one to arrive at the center and she could get her mind on her role as a volunteer. It was time to focus on someone else's problems, not her own.

A city employee had arranged the room as she'd asked with one long table down the middle of the area. A CD player was plugged into a socket, and Rosalie slipped in a children's disc of cheery songs. She wanted this activity to be fun.

She covered the table with a plastic tablecloth and began taking items from the carton she'd brought with her. Each child would have his own scrapbook, paste and safety scissors. She spread magazines, catalogues, ribbon, buttons, stickers, markers and other assorted craft supplies over the surface.

When the children arrived, Rosalie explained their project. "Tonight we're going to make a special book all about the person you've been missing." She peeled and stuck a name card on each scrapbook and told the children to print the name of the loved one who'd died.

"Make this book all about that person," she said. "Cut out pictures of things he used to do and things he liked, write down memories, make lists of words that make you think of this person. You can make your book silly or serious or a combination of both. You can write a story or a poem or draw a picture…anything you'd like."

During her training with the county mental health association, Rosalie had learned that previous theories about dealing with childhood grief didn't work well. Years ago, mental health workers were told that kids should be kept busy so they wouldn't dwell on the loved one who'd died. Now therapists believed that children needed to talk about their loss, needed to express their feelings. As the children prepared their scrapbooks, Rosalie walked around and let each one tell their stories and share experiences.

At the end of the evening, when they were cleaning up, one little boy said, "Miss Rosalie, did you make a book for your brother when he died?"

She'd told the children when she had first met with them that she had lost a very dear person in her family, and she missed him still. So she wasn't surprised when one of the kids brought up her experience. She smiled at the boy. "No, Josh, I didn't, but sometimes I wish I had."

"Do you talk about him?" a girl who'd lost a favorite uncle asked.

Rosalie thought about her answer. The truth was, she didn't talk about Ricky. She'd believed for so long that talking about him would only reopen the old wounds, so she'd kept her grief inside. Now, even though she knew better, the old habit was hard to break. And there wasn't really anyone to talk to. She answered honestly, "Not so much, Ginny. But I do talk *to* him. At least to his picture."

"Does that make you sad?" the girl asked.

"Sometimes, yes."

"You can talk to us about your brother if you want."

Her first instinct was to say what she always said: *No, I can't. I'm fine, really.*

But she didn't say that because suddenly she understood what had been missing for so long in her life. Maybe because Bryce had come home and forced her to look backward. Maybe because her own son was nearly Ricky's age now and so much like him. Maybe because she'd suddenly become wiser.

Whatever the case may be, as Rosalie packed up her carton and told the children goodbye, she knew that her time of grieving had never really ended because she'd never talked about Ricky. But now, the one person who'd known him as well as she did was back, and maybe it was time. If she was ever going to relive those precious years with Ricky, Bryce would be the one to listen and care.

She drove home in the gathering dusk and thought about the challenge ahead of her. Could she do it? Could she forget the awful vision of that horrible day long enough to confide in the person from whom she had kept her deepest secret? Was it fair to him to use him to lift the anchor of her grief? The blackest part of her heart seemed to claw at her chest in an attempt to break free of its prison. At the same time, exhilaration beat like butterfly wings in her chest. She could be rid of this awful weight of sorrow at last. Was it possible that the man who confessed to her that he "still missed him too," had come back to Whistler Creek so she could bare her soul? No, she told herself. Her soul would never be free as long as she kept this secret.

Gordon pulled up the driveway and stopped in front of Claudia's house. "We're back, safe and sound," he said. "Do you think your daughter is waiting up?"

Claudia pretended not to notice the light go off in Rosalie's bedroom window on the right side of the house. Nor did she comment on the face she'd just seen peeking through the blinds. "Oh, I'm sure she's been asleep for hours," she lied. "Would you like to come in for a cup of coffee?"

"I'd like that fine," Gordon said. "It's not late. Only 11:30."

Usually Claudia would have been asleep for over an hour. Again, not something she wanted to admit to Gordon. "No, it's not late. This big car of yours just eats up the miles faster than anything."

"I told you it wouldn't seem like a long way to Savannah," he said. "The Escalade makes an hour's trip seem like a few minutes. And the right assortment of music doesn't hurt, either."

"I'm really impressed with that satellite radio," Claudia said.

"Once you get used to having it, regular FM

stations seem dull by comparison." He got out of the SUV and walked around to open Claudia's door.

She could become accustomed to this gentlemanly attention. Throughout the evening Gordon had been concerned with her comfort. She'd selected all the stations on the fancy radio.

"Imagine driving all the way to Savannah for a meal," she said as they walked up the porch steps.

"I've always liked the Rusty Anchor Inn," he said. "There's no place better for fresh shrimp."

She stepped through the door, tossed her purse and sweater on the sofa and continued into the kitchen. "The whole evening was a real treat," she said, getting the coffeemaker started.

Gordon sat at the table. "Didn't you go out to dinner with your late husband?"

"Oh, sure. Every other Saturday night. We'd go to the Cracker Barrel out at the highway exit, and then sometimes end up at the movies."

She busied herself measuring the grounds so she wouldn't have to look at Gordon. How provincial she must have sounded talking about the Cracker Barrel after he had left a hundred-dollar bill folded in the check booklet at the Rusty Anchor. He'd tried to hide the denomination from her, but Claudia had always been aware of money and she couldn't help looking. She remembered the time when she fed her family of four for a week on less money.

"I love the Cracker Barrel," he said. "If it wouldn't make you feel like I was intruding on the private time you had with your husband, I'd like to take you there sometime."

She smiled. The evening had been too good to be true. Gordon Capps, former football star and tavern owner, always seemed to know the right thing to say. "I'd love that," she said, sitting across from him.

"It's a date." He put his hand on her forearm. "But this one isn't over yet."

"No, not yet. We still have to drink our coffee."

He grinned.

She blushed. Good heavens. She hoped Rosalie would stay in her room, because tonight, Claudia Campano was definitely getting a good-night kiss.

Chapter Thirteen

For the next two weeks, Rosalie concentrated equally on two tasks—preparing for the school year and fulfilling her promise to Bryce. While choosing fabric and accessories for his house, she kept her relationship with him as casual as possible, reminding herself almost constantly that she was merely keeping her word to a friend. Bryce, however, used their infrequent meetings as an opportunity to build on what had happened in his back garden. He found excuses to touch her arm, place a hand on her shoulder, lean close while evaluating decorating options. Rosalie resisted her growing, undeniable attraction and allowed her mind to go where it most wanted only in the dark hours of the night when she was alone.

If Bryce suffered from her obvious indifference to his advances, she was certain his frustration was no greater than her own. Truly, for Rosalie, being near Bryce was everything wonderful and horrible at the same time.

While Rosalie struggled to maintain an emotional distance from Bryce, romance of another kind was flourishing in the Campano household. Claudia and Gordon were now on a twice weekly schedule of going to dinner and the movies. Claudia personally delivered fresh produce to Cappy's Place at least once a week, and often her visits lasted long into the afternoon. Rosalie was happy for her mother and marveled at how Coach Capps's attention caused her mother to bloom.

Under Coach Benton's mentoring, Danny blossomed, as well. The two males seemed to grow closer each day. While Rosalie dreaded thinking that her son might be called upon to lead the Wildcats, Danny yearned for the chance to prove himself to his coach in a game. *His coach.* The sad irony of that label only increased Rosalie's guilt over the secret she kept.

So the days of summer passed slowly with Bryce and Ricky still occupying vital places in Rosalie's heart, equally strong, and, in their own ways, equally sad.

One Friday in mid-August, the week before school started, the teachers and staff were at the high school planning for the students' return. Bryce came in from the field house and found Rosalie in her classroom.

She looked up from lesson plans. "Hi. What's up?" Casual, friendly. Two old buddies sharing a break from their work.

"Rosie, can you go out to my place when you're done here? I've got practice, and my new appliances are being delivered today. I need someone there to let the driver in."

"I guess I could. I'll be done here in an hour or so."

He tossed his house key on her desk. "Thanks." He should have left, but he didn't. Instead he leaned on her desk, and looked down at her. "Are you ready for the kids to come in on Monday?"

"I am. After ten years of this, I should know what I'm doing."

"I'm sure you do. From everything I've heard, you're a great teacher."

She felt color rise to her cheeks. Funny how a harmless compliment from Bryce could affect her so. "When do you think you'll be home?" she asked.

"Suppertime anyway. Do you want to stay? I can fire up the grill."

She tapped her pencil on top of her planning book and tried to concentrate on what she'd last written. Looking into those deep blue eyes seemed like a quick trip to yes. It was Friday night. She had nothing to do.

"Can't," she said, erasing a doodle she'd scribbled earlier. "Some other time." They were two friends chatting, making tentative plans that might or might not happen. Perfectly natural. And yet unbelievably agonizing.

"Rosie, stay for dinner. It's ridiculous the way we've been dancing around…"

"Bryce, I really have to get back to this work, especially if you want me at your place this afternoon."

He stood straight. "Fine. Suit yourself." He walked out the door and called from the hallway. "Thanks for the favor."

She arrived at his house at three-thirty. When she walked in, she experienced the same feeling of accomplishment that swept over her whenever she visited the homey farmhouse. Her efforts were everywhere in evidence, in the warm plaid cushions on the maple couch, the rich burgundy of the curtains framing dark pine shutters. Pillows with duck and deer prints plumped the backs of each piece of furniture. Outdoor prints made the freshly painted tan walls come alive with the beauty of South Georgia.

"This room is so nice," she said aloud. "So perfect for Bryce." *And you, Rosalie.*

She sat in one of the inviting armchairs, picked up a book and began to read. Thirty minutes later, the truck arrived. Rosalie went outside and greeted Howie Delay, a man she'd known for years.

"Got some top-notch appliances here, Rosalie," he said.

She held the door as Howie and his helper carted in stainless steel appliances. They installed the stove and dishwasher, but when they tried to slide the refrigerator into place, they hit a snag. "Have you got an extension cord?" Howie asked. "The outlet is too far for the existing cord to reach. Be better if it's one of those heavy duty types."

"I'm sure Bryce has one somewhere," she said. She looked through drawers and cabinets and finally opened the pantry door. A heavy gauge orange cord was coiled on the top shelf. She took it down and gave it to Howie, but not before a box on the pantry floor caught her eye—an old, corrugated carton that appeared to have been opened many times. The tape on top was cracked and dry. On the outside were the initials WCHS. Whistler Creek High School?

She closed up the pantry and sat in a kitchen chair while the men finished.

"All done, Rosalie," Howie said. "Everything's turned on and running. We're taking off."

When they'd gone, Rosalie stared for several minutes at the pantry door. Wrestling with her conscience, she checked her watch. Bryce probably wouldn't be home for at least an hour. *No, Rosalie,* she said to herself. *It's none of your business.*

But if she was going to look, she'd better hurry!

She pulled the box onto the kitchen floor and sat down cross-legged to open it.

A musty garage smell wafted up from the contents as she began pulling out the significant mementos of Bryce Benton's past. And with them, some memories of her own.

Awards, citations, the embroidered letters he had earned in several high school sports. Copies of report cards, some good, some average. A few trophies.

And then there was Ricky. Much of the contents of the box was a testament to the two boys and the friendship they'd shared. Rosalie would have never suspected that Bryce was the type of person to save such minutia of his life. There were photos of the boys from childhood on. Pictures of the three of them, most Rosalie couldn't even remember being taken. On the backs Bryce had written their first names, the dates and the events. Rosalie recalled the county fairs, the first days of school, the bicycle marathon they'd all participated in for The Humane Society.

There were even pictures of the three of them on prom night, reminding her of the recent day when Bryce had said he'd hated Johnny Baxter.

One day before she had finally admitted that she'd always loved Bryce.

At the bottom of the box, buried as if symbolic of the tragedy of their past, there was a sort of memorial to Ricky. Rosalie scanned the photos of Ricky in his football uniform, his senior class picture, Ricky in his graduation gown. She smiled thinking of Roland Benton and how he had always seemed to have his camera at the significant moments of their lives. The Campanos rarely took pictures.

She set the photos aside and picked up a yellowed newspaper clipping. The headline made her head swim. *Local boy dies in freak accident at park.* She forced herself to read it. The story was more than an obituary. What happened to Ricky was news in Whistler Creek, not just a mention of a short life that ended tragically. The reporter covered her brother's seventeen years with words of praise for his accomplishments and sadness that his future was cut short.

Ricardo Campano is survived by his parents and his sister, Rosalie.

When a drop of water fell on the clipping, Rosalie realized tears were streaming down her face. She let them flow as she picked up the last paper in the box, a computer-generated letter dated one week after Ricky's funeral. With trembling fingers, she unfolded it.

Dear Ricky,

I wish I could send this to you, but I will just have to hope that you know I'm writing it. You Catholics believe in all this life-after-death stuff, so maybe you do know. Ha ha. Rosalie hates me now. I don't blame her. But I don't know what to do to make her know how badly I feel. She won't talk to me. I love her, Ricky. I always will. I am so sorry for what happened. I want to promise you that I will always take care of Rosie. I don't know if I will be able to do that. But I will try. I miss you, QB. I will never have a friend like you. Ever. Maybe

I'll become a Catholic so I'll know that I will see you again. You'll talk to me, won't you? See you in heaven, buddy.
Love,
Bryce
(I bet you're laughing at how I signed this.)

Sobbing now, Rosalie didn't hear the front door open. She didn't hear footsteps on the hardwood floors. The first she knew she wasn't alone was when Bryce said her name.

"Rosie…"

She gulped, dropped the letter and scrubbed her knuckles over her wet face. "Bryce, I didn't hear you. How long…?" She stopped, swallowed. Her throat burned.

He knelt down beside her. "What are you doing, Rosie?"

"I…I found this box. I'm sorry…."

He began clearing the photos and papers scattered around her, putting them carefully back in the carton.

She sat perfectly still, too exhausted to move,

too ashamed to speak. After he'd cleaned the clutter, she said, "I shouldn't have. It was wrong."

He carried the box back to the closet and reached down for her hands. "There's nothing there I wouldn't want you to see, Rosalie."

She placed her hands in his and let him lift her to her feet. "But these are your private memories."

"Yes, they are. But there's nothing in this box that I haven't tried to tell you about before. Maybe I should have showed you myself."

She sniffed, ran a finger under her nose. "Oh, Bryce, it's all so sad still."

He gathered her to his chest, ran his hands over her back. "It is, Rosie. It's sad."

She pressed her lips lightly against his neck and said, "I never realized how much you loved him."

He nodded. "Your blood ran in his veins, honey, but he was every bit a brother to me, too. It broke my heart when he died."

Her breath hitched with sobs again. Tears

soaked his shirt collar. He smelled of soap, fresh air and a little of sweat from his ride home in the truck. He was so real, so alive. "I'm so sorry, Bryce," she said again.

"For what, Rosie? What are you sorry for?"

"For not answering your letters, your phone calls. For not understanding. For not being there for you. For more than you can know...."

He continued to soothe her with his hands. His low voice reverberated in her ear. "Shh. It's okay, Rosie, it's okay."

"I loved you," she said.

"I know. I love you, Rosie. You've always been my girl."

She leaned back from him, looked into his eyes. "Do you love me now?"

He smiled. "You know I do." He cupped his hand around the back of her head. "You know what Ricky would be saying right now?"

"What?"

"That we're pinheads for letting all those years get away."

She chuckled. "He would say that."

"And he'd laugh out loud at how soft and mushy we're being now."

She smiled and realized it didn't hurt anymore. "Remember when he said he always knew we'd be together? Remember when he took credit for everything we were feeling back then?"

Bryce laughed softly. "Ricky took credit for everything good that happened to anybody. But the bad stuff? He'd back off and say, 'Don't look at me.'"

"He would, wouldn't he?" Rosalie ran her hand down Bryce's arm, relishing the sturdy comfort of the feel of him. "Remember when we went to the county fair and I threw up after riding on the Ferris wheel, and blamed Ricky for making me eat two caramel apples? He said it was all your idea."

Bryce smoothed his hand down her hair. "That was Ricky."

"He could really be a stinker. Remember when he…" She stopped, as an almost ethereal lightness came over her. She felt as if her feet could no longer connect with the floor. She was floating in Bryce Benton's arms, weightless at the same time he grounded her with his solid strength. She sighed deeply. So this was how it felt to be free.

He smiled down at her. "Have you forgiven me, Rosie? Is it over?"

"I forgave you years ago, Bryce," she said, and meant it. "But I never let go of the weight of grief. I never really believed I could."

He lowered his head and pressed his lips on hers. Warm, salty, generous lips that fed a spirit that all at once longed to soar above the confines of her eternal sadness. When she was dizzy with the taste and feel of him, he scooped her up in his arms. "I think we need to go to the bedroom, Rosie-girl. I think we need to celebrate life in this house."

Rosalie wrapped her arms around his neck and snuggled into his embrace. He set her down on the tan-and-green comforter she'd picked out herself and slowly, gently began to undress her. When he finished he slid back the covers and she settled on cool, new sheets. Bryce undressed quickly and immodestly, giving her a full and complete view of the man he had become. Muscled, lean, sculpted by hard work and training, he filled her mind and heart.

Before he got into bed with her, he took a foil package from the nightstand drawer. "I'm going to use this, Rosie, but I want you to know that if you and I had a child together, the last thing I would think is that it was a mistake." He opened the package. "But for now, for tonight..."

She turned her head just for a moment as he lay down beside her. But then he gathered her in his arms and kissed her deeply and thoroughly as his hands began the exploration of her body she'd been thinking about for weeks. What he'd just said should have fanned the fires of her guilt again, but she shut out any negative meaning. Maybe tomorrow, when she thought back, the old feelings would haunt her once more. But, as he'd just said, for now, for tonight, there was only Bryce. The sensual glide of his hands, the warm scent of his breath on her skin, the throbbing of him between her legs.

"I love you, Rosie," he said, his voice husky and deep, and she refused to think about anything but the joy he brought her.

Afterward she lay in his arms. Outside the window the sun had begun its descent and speared golden rays on the polished oak floor. The air conditioner hummed, chilling the room. But Bryce's arms were warm, his breathing as steady as the beat of her heart. "I finally feel like I've come home, Rosie," he said. "This house, my job, the town, but most of all you. I'm where I want to be."

She lay her hand on his chest, connecting to him, refusing to let the past intrude. Yes, tomorrow, maybe the day after, would be soon enough to deal with its consequences. Maybe this was a sign that she should keep the secret, start over from this point.

"Are you hungry?" he asked her. "That offer to grill steaks is still good."

She chuckled. "That reminds me. You haven't even looked at your new appliances. They're beautiful."

"I'm sure they are," he said. "But they probably look like they did on the showroom floor, so if it's okay with you, I'll stay right where I am another few minutes."

"It's okay with me."

He kissed her again, and the phone rang.

"Who could that be?" He checked the caller ID. "It's the county hospital."

Rosalie sat up, drawing the sheet over herself.

Bryce answered. His face registered shock. "What? How long ago?" He nodded once. "I'll be right there."

He returned the phone to the cradle. "I have to go, Rosalie. My dad's had another heart attack."

Chapter Fourteen

Rosalie left the farmhouse when Bryce did and arrived home at 8:30 p.m. Her mother and Gordon were at the kitchen table. Both had worried expressions on their faces.

Rosalie went to the refrigerator for a bottle of water. "Don't tell me," she said. "You heard already."

"Kitty from the beauty shop called me," Claudia said. "She was at the hospital visiting a friend when the ambulance brought Roland in." Claudia shook her head. "Isn't it awful? Poor Roland. How bad is it, do you know?"

"No, Mom, I don't. I was just with Bryce a few minutes ago when he was called to the hospital."

Rosalie couldn't ignore the I-told-you-so look that passed between her mom and Gordon.

"How is Bryce?" Gordon asked.

"Upset, worried."

Gordon nodded.

"I should call Marjorie," Claudia said. "We're not especially close, but at a time like this…"

"Why don't you wait, Mom?" Rosalie suggested. "Let's see what the prognosis is."

"Okay, you're probably right."

The next time Rosalie heard from Bryce was in the morning. Her phone rang at nine o'clock. She was on her second cup of coffee.

"Hope I didn't wake you," Bryce said.

"No. I didn't sleep well anyway. How is your father?"

"He's going to pull through. He's weak, and the doctors are telling him to rest. They performed a minor procedure last night, so they'll probably keep him in the hospital a few days."

"That's a relief. Were you there all night?"

"I took Mom home after Dad was out of surgery. Then I went back to my place. I got a couple hours of sleep."

"Where are you now?"

"At the hospital. I planned on staying and asking Cappy to handle practice, but Dad told me to go on. He said he's fine. So I guess I'll head over to the field house. We have our first game in six days you know."

Oh, yes, she knew. All Danny had been talking about was the possibility of getting in that game. "Right. I haven't forgotten," she said. "Look, Bryce, if there's anything I can do..."

"It's all good for now, Rosie. Just knowing that you're there is enough."

"Call me if you need a favor. Anything."

"I will... And Rosie?"

"Yes?"

"We didn't get a chance to talk after...well, and now's not such a good time either, but I want you to know how much last night meant to me."

Somehow, in the face of Bryce's emergency, smiling didn't seem appropriate, but Rosalie couldn't help herself. "Me, too," she said.

"I spent an odd few hours here at the hospital. Worrying about Dad, thinking about you, still feeling what I'd felt just a short time before. I'm not a guy who gets a real good handle on his emotions, but you made me a happy man last night in spite of what I faced here."

She sighed into the phone. How completely she understood what he was saying. While she'd been concerned for Roland Benton, she hadn't been able to stop thinking about what she and Bryce had shared. Their lovemaking had held all the excitement and anticipation of their youth, but so much more. The tenderness and caring that comes with maturity, the hope and faith that comes with starting over.

There was no putting it off. Rosalie had to make a decision soon, and it would be the most important one of her life. How could she truly start over with Bryce as long as the secret existed between them? So…should she tell him about Danny and risk hurting him and tearing apart the fragile ties they'd formed? The truth could break his heart. Or should she take the secret to her grave, and build a life with Bryce from this day forward? Maybe that was a sin. She supposed it was, but if she chose that direction, she hoped God would forgive her. But could she ultimately forgive herself? Some sins were too big to live with.

"Rosie? You still there?"

She squeezed her eyes shut and let his voice comfort her. "Yes, I'm here."

"You haven't changed your mind have you? We're still good?"

For now. "Oh, yes, Bryce, we're good. The best."

"Okay, then. I'll talk to you later."

She hung up and headed down the hall to get dressed. Just now, hearing Bryce's voice so confident, so trusting; how could she destroy that trust by telling him the truth? How could she not? The irony of her predicament brought tears to her eyes. Being completely honest could mean he'd never trust her again.

An hour later, the phone rang. Rosalie ran into the house after exercising Dixie and grabbed the phone.

"Rosalie? This is Marjorie Benton."

Rosalie's hand tightened on the phone. She sat in the nearest chair. Mrs. Benton had never called her before. "Mrs. Benton," she said. "I'm sorry to hear about your husband's heart attack. Bryce tells me he's expected to recover."

"That's what the doctors say. But naturally I'm worried about him."

"Of course. Is there something I can do for you?"

Marjorie paused, cleared her throat. "Not for me, Rosalie. But apparently for Roland."

"Oh?"

"He wants to see you. I can't imagine why, but he asked that I call you."

"I must admit I'm surprised."

"Can you come to the hospital?"

"I'll be there right away."

"I'll tell Roland you're coming. And Rosalie…?"

"Yes?"

"Don't agitate him."

Rosalie took a calming breath. "I'll certainly do my best not to, Mrs. Benton."

Rosalie arrived at the hospital a half hour later. She stopped outside Roland Benton's room, knocked softly and opened the door. Marjorie Benton stood up from a chair by the bed and came across the linoleum floor.

"Remember what I told you," she whispered. "Don't upset him."

Rosalie bit her bottom lip to avoid saying something that would make a tense situation worse.

"Rosalie," Roland said from his bed. "I'm so glad you came. Come over here, please."

She approached the bedside. "How are you doing, Mr. Benton?" Her former employment hierarchy at Benton Farms was probably the reason, but she couldn't fathom calling either of the Bentons by their first names.

"They say I'll live," Roland said. "And I fully expect to."

He turned his attention to his wife who hovered at the end of the bed. "Why don't you go to the cafeteria and get some breakfast, Marjorie?"

"I'm not hungry, dear," Marjorie said. "With Bryce gone to his practice, I'd just as soon…"

"Please, Marjorie. Everything will be fine. Just give us a few minutes, perhaps a half hour."

Marjorie paused a moment before picking up her purse and leaving the room. She gave Rosalie one last warning look.

"Don't mind her, Rosalie," Roland said when they were alone. "She fusses way too much."

"She's worried about you," Rosalie said.

"Yes, she is. But I've decided to make some changes in my life, with my goal being to stick around for a good while longer."

Rosalie didn't know what to say to that, so

she waited until Roland asked her to sit in the single chair the room offered. "We need to talk," he said.

"What's this about, Mr. Benton?"

"Why don't we start by cutting the formality, Rosalie? Please call me Roland."

"All right."

He smiled and she sensed he was trying to put her at ease. "You know, Rosalie," he said, "that facing one's mortality brings about a certain clarity that might otherwise go undiscovered."

"I imagine it would."

"I'm speaking of the decision we all made fifteen years ago. I'm sure you remember that night in our kitchen when we decided the fate of your and Bryce's child."

Of course she remembered. She'd only thought of it every day of her life since. "What are you trying to say?"

"Rosalie, do you recall seeing me at many of Danny's games over the years? From his first attempts at T-ball, to Little League and finally to his pitching success with his middle school team."

She had seen Roland in the bleachers on occasion, thought it perhaps relevant in light of their connection, but since he hadn't pursued a relationship with his grandson, she had never considered his presence a threat. "Yes, I did."

"I wasn't there out of a love for baseball," he said. "I was there because of the bond I felt with a boy I was never at liberty to acknowledge."

"We all agreed that it would be best—"

He held up his hand. "I know what we agreed, and a lot of good came out of that decision. You achieved your dream of becoming a teacher. Danny was raised in a home filled with love and support."

The first tingling of alarm snaked down Rosalie's spine. "Don't forget that Bryce went on to achieve his goals, as well."

"True, but now he's back, and I believe he's here to stay." He slid his hand across the blanket as if he were going to reach out to her.

"I know, too, that you and my son have been seeing a lot of each other."

"We have. That's not so unusual since we used to be friends."

He chuckled. "I'm not much of a betting man, but I would stake a few dollars on your relationship being more than friendship. It seems that things between you and Bryce may have come full circle, and that makes me happy for both of you."

Rosalie didn't respond to his accurate analysis, but she faced him squarely. "Where are you going with this...Roland?"

"I'm tired of living in the dark," he said. "I want to acknowledge my grandson, in the open, in the light. I want a relationship with him that goes beyond speaking to him at the warehouse or seeing him in town. He's my flesh and blood, Rosalie..."

"Stop right there," Rosalie said. She closed her eyes for a few seconds to try to quell the rash beating of her heart. She still didn't know what she would do. "Mr. Benton, you can't suddenly decide to go back on what we decided over fifteen years ago."

"Why not?" Roland pushed himself up in bed. "Things change, Rosalie. Circumstances change. Danny no longer has a grandfather to guide him."

"He has me."

"Yes, and no one would question your love for him, your role as his mother. He's grown into a fine young man, but he might agree that something is missing in his life, something that all of us have the power to fix. I think it's time to tell him the truth."

"I don't know," Rosalie said. "Hearing this now…" The consequences she'd thought about for weeks were still unbearable. She tried to find the words to complete her thought. "Danny would feel betrayed, manipulated."

"He's not a child anymore. And he might surprise all of us with his capacity to understand. He already has a relationship with Bryce."

"One that I tried to avoid from the start."

"But don't you see, Rosalie? You couldn't

avoid it. Call it fate if you will. Despite all your pleading, Danny did what he wanted. He and Bryce have developed a mutual respect for each other. I think this is a sign that those two should be given the chance to be what they were intended to be—father and son."

Marjorie's warning flitted briefly through Rosalie's mind, but she dismissed it. "This is all so you can call yourself a grandfather?"

She was so close to accusing Roland of trying to fulfill his own selfish desires, but in reality, Rosalie knew it was she who was the selfish one.

His tone remained calm. "I don't know how many good years I have left, but I want to make the best of the ones I have. I want to make my grandson a part of my family, my legacy."

"Your legacy? Is this about inheritance? That's not what is important. We're dealing with people's feelings and emotions."

He sighed. "I've upset you, and I'm sorry. This is about three men, connected by blood and love and duty. It's about stopping the lie, starting over, doing what's right." His eyes grew moist. "I want to be free to love him, Rosalie. That's the crux."

Rosalie's gaze darted to the machines monitoring Roland's condition. She didn't understand all the graphs and numbers, but his heartbeat appeared steady, the lines regular.

Roland patted her hand; it was the first time he'd touched her. "I'm fine. Quit looking at the damn screens."

She almost smiled. "Your wife will kill me..."

"She hasn't killed *me* in all these years, so I think you're safe."

They sat in silence a few moments until Roland said, "Think about it, Rosalie. Think about what would be best for Danny. Think about what Bryce and I, and yes, even Marjorie, could bring to his life." He paused, staring intently at her. "Will you do that?"

He made it sound so simple, and maybe to a man like Roland it was. But he couldn't know how all last night and again this morning Rosalie had struggled with her decision. She wanted a life with Bryce. Maybe they would have other babies and then all would be well. But inside she knew that was false hope with no foundation in reality. A future could not be built on a lie.

"Rosalie? Will you think about it?"

She wanted to say no, to take the easiest path. But what he'd said touched the deepest part of her heart. And her mind. Her lie was the roadblock to her happiness. And maybe Roland was right about Danny. She couldn't deny him a family that would love and support him, be there if something happened to her. A child could never be loved by too many people.

She stood and started to speak. "I…"

Marjorie came into the room, a cup in her hand. "I've brought you some coffee, dear," she said to her husband. "A touch of cream but no sugar."

"Thank you." He looked at Rosalie. "I appreciate your coming, Rosalie. We've had a lovely visit. Thanks again for all you've done to help Bryce get settled in his new house."

She nodded. "I wish you a speedy recovery." After a brief goodbye to Marjorie, she left the room.

Chapter Fifteen

Bryce rolled down the window on his truck to let in the late afternoon breeze. At the same time he kept the air-conditioning on full blast. Wasteful? Yeah, maybe, but after hours on the practice field in the hot sun, he didn't care.

Halfway to his house, he pressed the number one button on his cell phone's speed dial which he'd recently assigned to Rosalie. She answered promptly.

"Hey, Rosie, how has your day been?"

"Fine. Ran some errands, worked at the stand."

"And visited my father," Bryce added.

There was a slight pause before Rosalie acknowledged. "Yes, I guess he told you."

"That was really nice of you, Rosie. I know Dad appreciated it."

"I was happy to do it," she said. She waited another few seconds before saying, "Danny got home from practice a while ago. He said everything's going well."

"Absolutely. The guys are tense, anxious, but as prepared as they're going to be. I think we're ready for Friday night's home field opener."

"Good for you."

"Say, Rosie, I'd like to get together tonight…"

"That sounds nice, b—"

"Sure does, but here's the thing. I'm pretty much buried in responsibility. After I go home and shower I'm going to the hospital. Then I promised to take Mom out for a late dinner."

"Oh. That's all right."

Did she sound almost relieved? Bryce shrugged off his momentary doubt.

"I have plenty to keep me busy," Rosalie said. "Don't give it a second thought."

"Are you kidding? After last night, I've given you…us…much more than second thoughts."

An uncomfortable length of time passed before she said, "Well, of course, I have, too."

"Let's plan on Sunday night. We can go out to dinner, maybe to a place out of town if you want to keep our relationship under wraps for a while, and then come back here."

"You know I'd love to, but school starts the next morning."

"Yeah. And?"

"I have some finishing touches to put on my opening day handouts. And then there's Danny. Every year Mom and I take him out to dinner on the night before the first day of school. He gets to pick the place. Last year he picked Chili's in Valdosta, and I expect that will top his list this year, too."

"I see." He wondered why she didn't include him. Maybe she didn't want Danny to know that his mom and his coach had gotten close.

Didn't make much sense to Bryce. The kid was sure to find out soon enough. Bryce certainly didn't want to keep his feelings for Rosalie a secret.

"It's a tradition, Bryce. I can't disappoint him."

"No, you wouldn't want to do that."

"Thanks. We'll see each other on Monday, I'm sure."

Bryce swung into his driveway. "Rosie, is everything okay? My mother didn't say anything to upset you today, did she? I know she was in Dad's room when you stopped by."

"No. She was perfectly lovely. Everything is fine."

He wanted to believe her, but when he disconnected, Bryce couldn't ignore a niggle of doubt. What had happened this morning? His father had mentioned Rosalie's visit, said they had had a nice chat. Rosalie had wished him a speedy recovery. All appeared perfectly normal. And yet…

The opening of school didn't help to eliminate Bryce's misgivings. On Monday after school he stopped at Rosie's classroom and told her that he was booked up that evening with a meeting with Cappy, his trainers and his team manager. Once again she was understanding to the extreme. On Tuesday he stopped by again and tried to suggest they get together later. She informed him that she was busy the next two nights at the Brighter Day Center. He didn't even try for Thursday night. He was bringing his father home from the hospital that day. And besides, the game was the following day, and he knew where his head would be.

If his relationship with Rosalie had hit a roadblock, he didn't need to make things worse by having his thoughts wander in all directions when he was with her. He decided to get through game night and then use the weekend to make up for whatever he might have done to upset Rosalie. Of course he'd have to get her to tell him first. And he knew one thing for sure. He wasn't going to let her shut him out. Not this time. Not when they'd come this far.

He saw her in the gymnasium bleachers on Friday afternoon during the school pep rally. When he spoke to the student body, he felt her gaze on him, and convinced himself that she was sending vibes of support that his words would touch the right note of fervor and fair gamesmanship. Public speaking wasn't Bryce's strong suit. When he finished, she smiled down at him. Then she cheered along with the rest of the school when the players were introduced.

He caught up to her in the hall afterward. "Tonight, Rosie," he said, leaning close to her. "Win, lose or draw, you and I are going to get together, either with a beer to cry in or a bottle of champagne to toast to victory."

"Looking forward to it," she said. "And I hope I get to bring the champagne."

He allowed himself to bask in relief for a few seconds. Everything was okay. "Give me an hour or so after the game to wrap things up with the players and then come over."

She nodded.

"You'll be in the stands, won't you?" he asked.

"Are you kidding? I wouldn't miss it. Mom and I will be there early to get a seat on the fifty-yard line." She started to walk away but stopped and turned back to him. "About Danny…"

He smiled at her. "He's ready, Rosie. I won't put him in unless the situation calls for it, but don't worry. The quarterback is the most protected guy on the squad."

"I'm just worried because I know Danny can be very persuasive. And he really wants in this game."

"Yeah, I've seen that. And he's worked hard and earned his chance. But I have a hunch we'll stick with our number one quarterback on opening night."

"Okay. I'll quit worrying."

He knew that wasn't possible.

She smiled at him. "Good luck, Coach."

He was surrounded by fellow teachers also giving him good wishes, and Rosalie was soon down the hall and around the corner. And Bryce knew as soon as he ran onto the field with his players later that night, he'd be glancing up at the fifty-yard line.

Rosalie and Claudia arrived at the game forty minutes early and secured their seats on the fifty-yard line. Rosalie watched players from both teams perform calisthenics on the field for a few minutes before going back to the locker room for what she assumed was a last pep talk from their respective coaches. She could easily have picked out Danny among the Wildcat squad even if his jersey number hadn't identified him. Taller than most of his teammates, he was also considerably thinner. Not uncommon for a quarterback but no match for the bruisers on the other team whose goal was to stop him. Rosalie was thankful again that Bryce said he probably wouldn't put Danny in.

"Doesn't our boy look handsome in his uniform?" Claudia said when Rosalie pointed Danny out.

Rosalie agreed. "I'm just counting on that

uniform staying clean. I don't want to see any grass stains on it."

Claudia patted her hand. "Don't fuss, now. Everything is going to be fine. Gordon says Danny is quite capable."

Claudia's capacity for moving forward had always amazed Rosalie. And made her just a little bit envious.

By the time the game started at eight o'clock, the bleachers were filled with Wildcat supporters. On the other side of the field, there were almost as many Eagles fans from the high school twenty miles away. The Wildcats won the coin toss and elected to receive. And from that point on, the air bristled with cheering voices, applause and the thud and grunts of husky young men ramming into each other.

The Wildcats took an early lead and never looked back. With each first down, Danny hollered from the bench. When points were scored, he stood up and pumped his fist and congratulated his teammates when they returned to the sideline.

Rosalie admired his enthusiasm, since she knew how badly he wanted to get in the game. Even accepting that his chances were slim to none, he continued to bolster his team's spirit. And when the Eagles took a time-out with only fifty-eight seconds left in the game, and the score was thirty-one to twelve in favor of the Wildcats, Rosalie sighed with relief. She'd gotten through game one without fainting or crying or chewing her fingernails.

"You want to go soon?" Claudia asked. "We're obviously going to win, and if we leave before the last play, we can avoid traffic in the parking lot."

"I'm going to stay until the end," Rosalie said. "You can go if you want, but Danny knows where I'm sitting." *And so does his coach.* "He'll probably look up when the final whistle blows. I should be here."

"Are you coming home?" Claudia asked.

"No, not for a while." Rosalie could only think of her promise to Bryce and that bottle of champagne she said she'd bring. And the confession she had decided to make tonight. The rest of her life hinged on the next couple of hours. She prayed the celebration wouldn't be ruined when she told him the truth about Danny. She had considered her decision from every angle and knew this was the right thing to do. She loved Bryce now more than ever, but keeping that love alive did not mean living with a lie.

"Rosalie! Rosalie!"

She turned when she felt her mother tugging on her blouse sleeve. "What is it, Mom?"

"Look. I think Bryce is putting Danny in the game."

"No, he wouldn't…"

Words strangled in her throat. There was her son, standing next to Bryce. Bryce's right hand was on Danny's shoulder. He was speaking into his ear, gesturing with his left hand. Then he clapped Danny on the back and sent him onto the field.

"What is he doing?" Rosalie said. "Fifty-eight seconds! He's putting Danny in now? He doesn't have to!"

Claudia stared down at the field. "Don't they sometimes do that, Rosalie? Let the second-string guys in when the game is a sure thing? I know the backup quarterback used to go in for Ricky when the score was so lopsided."

And as if she could combat Bryce's surprise move with one simple rationale, she cried, "Yes, but that kid wasn't Danny!" She cupped her hands around her mouth, ready to scream, ready to tell Bryce that he was breaking his word.

"Don't do it," Claudia said, gently pulling Rosalie's hands from her face.

All her discussions with Bryce swam in her mind now. How could he? But then, he really hadn't given his word, had he? Hadn't he always cleverly danced around the issue, giving excuses, making blanket statements that could be taken either way. Yes, clever Bryce. He'd never really given his word.

She made herself watch as the two teams

CYNTHIA THOMASON

305

faced off on the line of scrimmage. She prepared herself for the longest fifty-eight seconds of her life.

The center snapped the ball. Danny caught it and handed off to a running back who ran quickly out of bounds, stopping the clock. The play ended. Only a few seconds left. Danny looked to the bench, signaled his coach. Bryce nodded.

What did that mean? What was Bryce agreeing to?

Danny again received the ball from the center, stepped back, raised his arm to throw. Players all around him dug into the turf, fell onto each other and blocked tacklers. All but one. A kid who looked to be twice Danny's size found a hole in the mass of bodies and bolted through.

He head-butted Danny directly in his gut. The ball went forward and Danny went down, the big opposing tackle landing on top of him. And Rosalie gulped in the last breath she would take for many torturous seconds.

A referee blew a whistle and the game ended.

The stands erupted in cheers. The Wildcats chest-pumped and back-slapped each other and their coach.

And the announcer's voice broke through all the excitement and chilled Rosalie to the marrow of her bones. "There's a Wildcat player down. It's number twelve, the young freshman quarterback, Danny Campano."

The crowd hushed. The players all turned toward their fallen teammate. The trainer rushed onto the field followed by Bryce.

Rosalie barreled through the crowd and down the steps to the fence that separated spectators from the field. Her fingers gripped the wire. Her eyes burned. "Danny!" she cried.

But Danny didn't move.

The trainer signaled for an open four-wheeled vehicle to come onto the grass. Danny was loaded into it and taken off the field. Rosalie brushed off her mother's hand and raced through the crowd to the athletic building where she would find her son.

* * *

Rosalie burst through the double doors of the field house and had made it halfway down the hall to the locker room before she was stopped.

"Hold up, Rosie. He's fine."

A strong hand gripped her upper arm. She spun around to stare into Bryce's face. He was still wearing his black-and-gold Wildcat shirt and his coaching shorts.

She tried to wrench her arm free. "Let me go!"

"No. I can't do that."

She was only marginally aware of the effort he was taking to keep his voice level.

"He's okay, Rosie," Bryce said. "He's sitting up on a bench in the locker room. In a minute he'll be in the shower with the other guys."

She tried again to loosen his grip. He only tightened his hold. "I want to see him, Bryce."

"Trust me for once, will you, Rosie? I'm telling you he's fine."

"He wasn't even moving!"

"He never lost consciousness. The doctor isn't

even ordering any tests. Rosie, he only had his bells rung."

"Bells rung? What does that even mean?"

"You know what it means. You've heard the term your whole life. He just had the wind knocked out of him. That can cause immobility and dizziness. But it passes."

"When did you get your medical degree?" she shouted at him.

He drew in a long breath. "It happens to at least one player in nearly every game, Rosalie. Danny is fine. I just left him."

She narrowed her eyes, tugged against his hand. "Let me see for myself."

"You can't go in the locker room, you know that. Do you want to embarrass the kid possibly for the rest of his life? Not to mention embarrassing yourself."

"Do you think I care about being embarrassed?" she said. "I want to see him."

"And I'm telling you that would be a mistake. If you'll wait outside, I'll go in and tell him you're here. When he's dressed he can come out."

She released a trembling sigh, and he loosened his grip on her arm. She defiantly tugged her sleeve back into place. But she didn't dart away. "How could you do this, Bryce? How could you put him in the game?"

"Because he's earned the chance to be in it. He wanted in. He wanted it as much as I've ever seen any kid want anything. He deserved his shot."

"He's not *any* kid," she blasted him. "He's *my* kid, and we had a deal."

"No, Rosie, we didn't. You made a demand and I chose not to follow it." He paused, his eyes suddenly sad. "I couldn't."

She knew he was right. And that made her position groundless. She'd known the chance she was taking in signing the parental consent form. She'd known it and signed it anyway. If anyone was to blame, she had only to look in the mirror. But, damn it, Bryce couldn't get off scot-free.

Bryce put his hand on her arm again, this time gently. "Don't you think I realize whose kid he is?" he asked. "I've thought about that every day since Danny signed up. I know how you feel, but I have to treat him like I would any other boy who wants to play football. And that's what he is, Rosie. A football player, a member of a team, one who has worked his guts out on the practice field."

"I can't believe you could be so callous, so indifferent about our son…" She blurted the words before she knew what she was doing.

She stopped, bit her bottom lip until she tasted blood.

"What did you say, Rosie?" he said.

She shook her head. No, he couldn't have heard. It was a slip of the tongue.

Bryce grabbed her arms again, shook her. "Say it again, Rosalie."

She gasped, closed her eyes to his penetrating gaze that seemed to burn into the conscience she'd tried so long to ignore.

"Is Danny my son?"

Weakness threatened to buckle her knees. She hadn't planned to reveal her secret this way, but Bryce's words had somehow opened the door and the truth swept through despite her best intentions. She swallowed and answered him.

"Yes."

He dropped his arms. "Danny is mine?" he said in a voice barely above a whisper. "But his birthday. I checked his records."

"Wh…when he was born, I changed the date on everything but his official birth certificate."

"Oh, God, Rosalie."

She wanted to hide, to crawl through a crack in the floor, to evaporate into the air. What she'd just admitted was unbelievably wrong on so many levels.

She risked a look into Bryce's face. His expression was a tight mask of shock and betrayal. His eyes blinked rapidly as he fought to understand, make sense of the inconceivable. "Danny is my son," he said again, louder this time.

Movement in the corner of her eye drew Rosalie's attention to the door to the locker room. Her son stood there in socks and his uniform, head bare, his hair tumbling onto his forehead. His eyes widened in horror.

"What the hell, Mom, is that true? Is what Coach just said for real?"

Chapter Sixteen

"Danny… Oh, God, sweetie." Rosalie felt as if she'd just been plunged into an ice-cold lake. Her arms trembled. Her legs were unsteady as she took a few steps toward her son.

"Don't come near me," he said.

"You weren't supposed to hear that."

"Yeah, right. I guess I wasn't supposed to hear it for the last fifteen years, too."

She reached a hand out to him. "Give me a chance to explain." Wasn't that what everyone said when caught in such a damnable lie? And like most everyone else, Rosalie had no idea how she would reason away what her son had heard. But she needed time to connect with him.

"Just answer the question, Mom. What Coach said, is it true?"

"Danny…"

"Damn it, Mom! There are only two answers. Yes or no."

A few of Danny's teammates, obviously drawn by the commotion, gathered in the doorway to the locker room, some of them shirtless, in jeans, their hair wet from their showers.

And Rosalie stood as one separate from many, knowing that her life would never be the same. Some of these boys were in her English classes. Some belonged to her church. All of them were in her town, had parents Rosalie considered friends. They looked from her to their coach, to their teammate.

No one spoke. It was as if they were all waiting for Rosalie to break the ice that had frozen them together in this awful moment.

Danny's face, his beautiful face so like

Ricky's, was contorted in a grimace of pain. Or perhaps it was hate. Rosalie had no choice but to answer him. He was enough of a man now that he wouldn't accept being put off. She nodded once. "Yes, Danny, it's true."

He glared at Bryce with scorn almost equal to the look he gave his mother. "Did you know this before right now?"

Bryce glanced quickly at Rosalie. The shake of his head was almost imperceptible. His mouth formed the word *no,* though he didn't make a sound.

Danny emitted a noise like a low growl. He raked his fingers through his hair and bent over double as if his stomach hurt. Rosalie rushed to him. He stood straight and held up his palm. "Stay away from me."

She halted a few feet from him. "Are…are you hurt?"

He laughed, a low guttural noise she'd never heard him make before. "Hurt? Yeah, I'm hurt. I'm hurt that you've lied to me my entire life.

You told me my father was a guy you hardly knew. That he had no interest in being a father."

"I had my reasons, Danny."

"What reason could you have had to turn *my* life into one big lie?" He spun around when one of his teammates coughed. "Are you all enjoying this?" he said.

Shocked stares answered him.

"Get back inside and quit listening to what isn't your business. I don't want my stupid life…" He choked on his next words and covered his mouth with his hand. A sob sputtered through his fingers.

The other boys slowly ambled back inside the locker room.

And Rosalie could truly feel her heart break. A pain shot through her chest, threatening to cut off her air. She forced in a slow, agonizing breath.

"Danny, let's go home," she said. "We'll talk. I'll make this right. I swear I will."

He dropped his hand and stood straight. When he looked at her, there was nothing in his eyes but a black void. "I'm not going any-where with you."

"Don't say that. You have to go with me. I'm still your mother. You have to come home."

He stood silently for a moment, breathing heavily. After what seemed an eternity, he said, "I have to have a parent responsible for me, right?"

"Yes, you do."

He looked at Bryce. "Can I go home with you, Coach?"

Rosalie flattened her hand over her heart, a useless attempt to still the erratic beat in her chest. "Don't do this, Danny."

He reacted as if she hadn't spoken. "Coach?"

Bryce stared at Rosalie. She knew he hadn't had time to process what he'd just learned. Maybe when he had the chance to listen to her, he would look at her again the way he had just a few hours ago. Not like he did now, with shock and bitterness and contempt. Or maybe he never would again.

"Danny's idea might be best for tonight,"

Bryce said. "I'll take him home with me. We all need some time."

Rosalie's instinct was to fight, to wrap protective arms around her child and walk with him out of this nightmare. She started to step toward him again but felt a hand on her back. She turned and looked into her mother's eyes.

"Let's go home, honey," Claudia said. "You come with me."

Rosalie didn't know how much Claudia had heard. Obviously enough. She closed her eyes and gathered enough strength to let her mother lead her away. When they got to her car, Rosalie's cell phone rang. Her heart lurched. Her hand was trembling so fast she could hardly read the digital screen.

It wasn't Danny. She connected. "What is it, Bryce?"

His voice was clipped, short. "Just one question. Who knew about this at the time you were pregnant?"

"Let's not do this tonight…"

"Who, Rosalie?"

She looked at her mother in the passenger seat, and said, "Only five of us. Me and our parents."

He disconnected before she could tell him to take good care of their son.

Bryce waited in his office until the team had all left and Danny had taken a shower. Then together the two of them headed for his truck. Bryce struggled to find words—but any that came to mind sounded lame or shallow or forced. What could he say when he was still as confused and shocked as Danny was? Danny walked along silently beside him, his head bent, his eyes on the asphalt. He got in the passenger seat and buckled up.

Bryce started the engine and looked over when a safe topic occurred to him. "You hungry?"

Danny shrugged one shoulder. "I can't believe I am, but yeah, I could go for a cheeseburger." He reached in his jeans pocket. "I've got my own money."

Bryce almost smiled. "Never mind. I think after fifteen years I can treat you to a cheeseburger."

"Are you going to get one?"

"No." The thought of food made Bryce's stomach revolt. "But if it's okay with you, I think I'll have a beer when we get to my place."

"Why wouldn't it be? It's your life. Your house."

Bryce had wondered if the kid held any resentment toward him. Apparently he did, and Bryce would have to deal with it somehow.

After a mile, they reached the outskirts of town and Bryce turned into a Burger King. "This okay?"

"Sure. Can you order me a Whopper with cheese?"

Bryce requested the sandwich, large fries and a large soft drink. He passed the bag to Danny and the kid dug in. Bryce lowered his window and set his elbow on the door hoping the breeze would revive him enough to make his numb brain function again. At least feeding the kid was a good excuse not to have to talk.

He had a son, and he didn't know what to do about it. A few hours ago, he had a girl-friend. No, Rosie had become much more than that. And now he didn't know what the hell to do about her. He tried to find a sympathetic thought for her in his mind, but none would come.

The Whopper was history by the time Bryce drove past the Campano house. Lights were on in every room. He recognized Cappy's SUV in the drive behind Rosalie's car.

A mile further on, Bryce pulled into his long drive. "You ever been back here to the house?" he asked Danny as he drove up the recently cleared lane.

"No. I know my mom has, though. You and her been seeing a lot of each other."

Bryce nodded thinking how all that might change now.

They went inside and Bryce headed for the refrigerator. He uncapped a beer and took a long swallow while trying not to look at the bottle of champagne he'd left chilling on the counter. He tried not to think about the steaks in the fridge or the salad he'd made.

When he came out to the living room, Danny was sitting on the newly reupholstered sofa. His teenage radar had obviously kicked in and he'd found the remote and turned on the TV. *Family Guy* played in the background.

Bryce sat in a chair, took another pull on the bottle. "We should talk, don't you think?" he said.

Danny shrugged. "You gonna tell me to forgive her? You gonna say she's my mom and all that bull?"

"No. Forgiving her is your decision. I can't make it for you."

Danny slurped soda from his nearly empty cup and stared at the television. "Yeah, well, you might have a reason to forgive her that makes it easier for you. Stuff you did fifteen years ago. Stuff you're probably doing with her now for all I know."

Bryce picked up the remote and muted the volume. He and his son might practically be strangers, but he couldn't let the kid cross the line like that. "You know something, Danny?" he said. "Both of us are going to have to navigate these waters we've suddenly found ourselves in. I've never been a father, and you've never had a father, but we've got to find a way to communicate without sniping at each other."

Danny plopped his feet on the coffee table and slumped into the sofa.

"I expect we've got to have some rules, you and me," Bryce continued. "And the first one is, you and I won't talk about anything personal that's gone on between your mother and me. If you want to talk about personal stuff between your mother and *you,* I'll listen."

"Like that's fair."

"Maybe it isn't, but one advantage of being the adult is the right to set some boundaries. That's the one I'm setting."

"Aren't you even mad at her?"

Damn. What an understatement. The one

thing Bryce had gotten a handle on since hearing he was a father was that he was damned angry. Furious. His anger was clawing inside his chest right now looking for a release. He took another gulp of beer, welcomed the cool slide down his throat. He set the bottle on the table, leaned forward and threaded his hands between his knees. "I'm really mad at her," he said.

Danny speared him a glance. "She lied to us both."

"I know. She did."

"So, are you going to forgive her?"

Bryce watched the silent screen for a moment, buying time. This was the important question. The biggie. If he heard her reasons for what she'd done, would they make a difference? "I don't know," he said honestly. "For keeping a secret like this, maybe not."

Danny nodded.

"But I need time," Bryce added. "Just like you do to digest what we found out tonight. As far as life's unforgettable moments, this ranks up there near the top."

"Yeah."

"I'll tell you this. The way she told me was gut-wrenching, but the news itself, well, I can't say that it's so bad. I've got a lot to figure out, though."

"Like how to go from coach to dad?"

"Like that."

Danny stared intently at him. "To tell you the truth, I don't know how to let you do that, or even if I want you to do that."

Bryce smiled. "To tell you the truth, I don't know, either."

Danny drummed his fingers on his knee for a minute and then said, "What'd you think of the game tonight?"

"I thought it was freaking fantastic. You?"

"Yeah, it was great. Thanks for putting me in."

"You earned it."

The muted TV held their attention for a

minute until Bryce said, "I've only got one bed. Are you okay with the couch?"

"Yeah, I can sleep anywhere."

"Okay, then. Turn up the volume. I like this show."

Rosalie sat at the kitchen table across from her mother and Cappy. Her forehead rested in one hand while the other was wrapped around a cold cup of coffee she hadn't touched. No one had said anything since Rosalie's last frantic pace around the room.

"Do you want me to warm up your coffee?" Claudia offered.

Rosalie raised her head, looked at the cup as if for the first time. "No, I'll do it." She stood, walked toward the machine on the counter and then detoured to circle the room once more. "I can't believe I just blurted it out like that," she said for what seemed like the hundredth time.

"Do you want something to eat?" Claudia said.

"No." She emptied her coffee into the sink and went to the brewer for a refill.

Cappy scooped some egg onto his toast. "This is really good. Nobody makes eggs and sausage like your mother."

Rosalie looked at him. "I can't eat."

Cappy set down his fork. "You know, ladies, there's something we're not even considering about this whole situation."

Both women stared at him.

"This could be a good thing." He paused. "What I mean is, it's never healthy to live with a lie. It starts by nibbling away at you until it threatens to swallow your insides. Nobody wants to live that way."

Rosalie thought of Roland Benton. He'd said almost the same thing from his hospital bed. And she'd finally decided to tell Bryce the truth. But her confession had come out horribly wrong. She leaned against the counter and took a sip of coffee.

"And this just happened a couple hours ago. We need to give these guys time to adjust."

"Gordon's right," Claudia said. "When Bryce was a youngster, I knew him almost as well as I knew my own kids. He was always a sweet boy, fair and honest. I think we need to give him some credit for looking at this from both sides."

Yeah, right. Rosalie blew out a breath. "Like he believes there even are two sides."

"Bryce is a good man," Cappy said. "I've seen as much evidence of that as anybody the last few weeks." He leaned back in his chair. "I don't know how all this started, why you all made the decision you made fifteen years ago. Hell, I don't have to know, but I expect Bryce should. Maybe once you tell him…"

"If he'll ever give me the chance," Rosalie interrupted.

Cappy gave her a sort of half smile. "I'm thinking maybe you could make him give you that chance."

The night in the Benton kitchen flashed through Rosalie's mind again, as it had so often since Bryce's return. What did Rosalie trade

Bryce's fatherhood for? So he could realize his dreams, live up to his potential? That's what she'd told herself that night. That's what she'd been telling herself ever since and convincing herself that it had been the right decision. She'd even talked herself into believing that if Bryce looked at the situation logically he would thank her for relieving him of responsibility he wasn't ready for. Somehow all that rationalization seemed like a crock now.

"And as for Danny…" Cappy said, cutting into her thoughts, "he'll come around. A boy needs his mother, and from what I hear you've been a darned good one. He won't hold a grudge long. At least that's what I believe."

At this moment, when the life she'd been living had cracked into pieces like a dropped china cup, Rosalie couldn't accept that either Bryce or Danny would ever forgive her. And even if by some miracle they did, there were other consequences to pay. The whole town would know the truth soon. She thought of the boys standing in the locker room door and imagined a spiderweb of gossip growing out of their innocent eavesdropping. "Mom, what time is it?" she asked.

"It's nearly twelve," Claudia said. "Why?"

"I'll bet half the town knows about this by now. I don't remember if my teaching contract has a morals clause, but if it does, I wouldn't be surprised if I got a call from the school board."

"That won't happen, honey," Claudia said. "Everyone is aware that you're a single parent, and these days that's no shame. The revelation of the father won't make any difference. If anything, it might stop the few stubborn tongues that have been wagging for all these years."

"I'm not so sure. And speaking of wagging tongues, I can't believe our own phone hasn't rung at least once since we've been home. You'd think someone in this town would want to be the one to tell you the news or confirm what they heard."

"That's true," Claudia said. "But don't worry about that telephone. You go on and try to get some sleep. I turned the ringer off two hours ago."

Cappy beamed at her. "See why I like your mother so much? Common sense in a pretty package. Can't beat that combination."

In spite of everything, Rosalie smiled.

Chapter Seventeen

After managing to log in a whopping two hours of sleep, Bryce blearily navigated the short hallway to his living room at 7:00 a.m. He stopped near the sofa and just stared at his son. He wasn't sure how he should be feeling about this boy he'd only known as his backup quarterback, but he was definitely feeling something unique. And it was strong and powerful and, well, warm.

Danny was sleeping on his stomach. One leg hung over the couch cushion practically touching the floor. One hand dangled over the sofa arm. The blanket Bryce had given him was twisted around his legs, and Danny's head was burrowed sideways in the pillow. Damned uncomfortable to Bryce's way of thinking, but the kid had said he could sleep anywhere. He made small snuffing noises of contentment.

Bryce remained transfixed a moment longer and then wandered into the kitchen. "Amazing," he said to himself. "I guess everything I've heard is true. Teenagers sleep like they haven't a care in the world." He filled the coffeepot. "I wish I could do it."

Did he wish he were a teenager again? The thought crossed his mind and he dismissed it, though he'd been mostly happy then. He wouldn't want to start over, he mused. Even as bleak as everything looked today, he was glad that the course of events led to this kid having an inroad into his life. Maybe, just maybe, the two of them could make this work.

What about the three of you, Bryce? he asked himself. He didn't have an answer for that one.

While he had his coffee, Bryce wrote a note.

Danny, when you wake up, there's cereal in the cupboard and milk in the fridge. I won't be long, but if you need anything, call me and I'll pick it up on my way back.

He started to sign "Coach" at the bottom and then added a line.

On second thought, call me when you get up whether you need anything or not.

He figured that's what parents did. Checked in. Heard their kids' voices.

After another long pause, he wrote "Coach" and his cell phone number. He left the note on the coffee table, locked the front door and got in his truck. In fifteen minutes he pulled into his parents' driveway. He parked behind his dad's car and went in the kitchen door.

Roland, in pajamas and bathrobe, was at the kitchen table, obviously following doctor's orders to take it easy. His mother was dressed in slacks and a matching shirt, her meticulously colored blond hair combed neatly into her short style, her makeup applied. Pancakes, the usual weekend fare, sizzled on the stove.

When they saw their son, each reacted. Roland muted the news channel on the television. Marjorie dropped her spatula, turned off the burner and stared with eyes as round as the pancakes she was preparing.

After a moment of silence, Roland said, "Congratulations on the win last night, son. I hope that will be the only one I'll have to miss."

Bryce stood just inside the doorway. "Thanks." He looked from one parent to the other. "I'm assuming that you've heard about the other development last night. The one that more or less makes a high school football victory pale in comparison, at least as far as I'm concerned."

Marjorie flattened her hand over her bosom. "Oh, Brycie, sit down, sweetheart."

"I don't feel like sitting," he said.

"Sit anyway, Bryce," Roland said in a tone he rarely used.

Bryce yanked a chair away from the table and sat. His mother retrieved the spatula and slid it under a pancake. If she offered it to him, he thought he'd scream. She gave it to his father.

Bryce rested his forearms on the table and glared at his father. He took a long breath and reminded himself not to let his hurt and anger explode in a shouting match that might affect his dad's health. Roland had only been home from the hospital for three days. But Bryce was determined that his parents would know just how deeply their actions fifteen years ago had devastated him.

"How's Danny?" Roland asked.

"How do you think?" *Sleeping soundly,* but Bryce didn't admit that. "He's at my house. He's pretty pissed at his mother."

Roland nodded. "This has to be tough on him. And you."

"It's no picnic," Bryce said.

"Then let's have at it, Bryce. Say what you came to say."

Just like that? His father was encouraging

him to jump into the reason behind the anger and frustration that was eating his insides. Well, okay.

"How could you, Dad?" Bryce began. "You knew that Rosalie was pregnant. You knew the baby was mine."

Marjorie made a mewling sound from the stove. Roland responded in a level voice. "Yes, we did."

"You knew how I felt about her."

"Yes. And we knew how she felt about you after what happened to her brother."

"She would have gotten over that."

"No, son, she wouldn't have," Roland said sadly. "Not then. Not for a long, long time."

Bryce wanted to argue that point, but he couldn't. He'd since learned that Rosalie would never completely get over what happened to Ricky—any more than he would. "But it was my baby," he said. "You should have told me. You should have given me the chance to make things right."

"It was one option we all discussed at the time," Roland said.

"Options? You all discussed options? What about the option that included the father? What about having him in the conversation?"

"You were gone, Bryce, honey," Marjorie said. "You had been in Texas for several weeks by the time we found out. You'd started your new life and were doing so well…"

He gave his mother a scathing look. How wrong she was. "So you just left me out of this decision because I shouldn't have been bothered with the little inconvenience of my own baby?" He snorted. "God forbid something like a baby and a marriage should interrupt Bryce Benton's rise to the pinnacle of his football career."

"We did consider your future, son," Roland said. "And believe it or not, it was Rosalie who brought up your goals."

"Like she wanted to raise a baby on her own?" Bryce said. "Come on, Dad, why would she want to do that? The Campanos weren't wealthy people…"

"That's exactly what she wanted to do," Marjorie said.

Bryce looked at his father for confirmation.

"Your mother's right," Roland said. "Rosalie didn't want you to know."

A few agonizing seconds ticked by while Bryce let this sink in, and then his father added, "She wouldn't have married you, son. She didn't want to. She made that clear."

Bryce stared at the kitchen clock. The numbers swam before his eyes. He cleared his throat. "She hated me that much?"

"I don't think she ever hated you, Bryce," his father said. "I just think her heart was broken, and you were so mixed up in how that happened that she couldn't get over it." Roland reached across the table and covered Bryce's hand with his. "The marriage would have been a disaster, son. Rosalie would have been bitterly unhappy. Would you have wanted that?"

No, of course he wouldn't have wanted Rosie

to be unhappy. But still, that didn't make the conspiracy that went on behind his back right today. No one, not his parents, not the woman he'd fallen in love with all over again, had the right to keep him from his flesh and blood. Bryce shifted on the chair, refocused on his father. "Tell me how it went down," he said. "When did you find out Rosalie was pregnant?"

Roland explained about the phone call from Enzo, the meeting that night around their kitchen table. He told Bryce how he immediately started for the phone to call him.

Everything would have been so different if that phone call had gone through, Bryce thought. He wouldn't have made the choice to marry Audrey. He might still be married to Rosalie today. They might have had other children. Bryce might have been the father he had always envisioned himself to be.

Or...he might have ruined Rosalie's life, made his son miserable, been working for the last fifteen years in the produce warehouse.

But that should have been his choice. His and Rosalie's.

Roland told him that Rosalie had stopped him from making that call, said she didn't want to get married because of what happened to her brother. Roland explained that Enzo wanted the wedding to take place because, "that's the way things were done in the old country."

But Rosalie had been adamant, Roland said. And so a compromise had been struck.

"What sort of compromise?" Bryce asked.

Marjorie came over to the table. "Your father and I paid for Rosalie's college education," she said. "That's what happened, so you don't have to make yourself miserable thinking that Rosalie struggled for years raising a baby while working to put herself through college. She came out of this just fine."

Bryce flinched at his mother's tone. Obviously she hadn't approved of this aspect of the plan.

Roland stared her into silence. "At first Enzo refused the offer. He was a proud man. But

Claudia supported us, and Rosalie was sensible enough to accept that we only wanted to give her and the baby a good start." He looked at his wife again, willing her to remain quiet. "Thank goodness she did," he said. "Rosalie is a good teacher, well respected. She made something of herself and, by the way, raised a fine son."

A pang of anguish squeezed Bryce's chest. He'd had nothing to do with making his son a fine person, and he resented the hell out of that. But he had to give Rosie credit for doing a damn good job.

"No one outside of the five of us knew who the father was," Roland continued. "After her freshman year, Rosalie came back to town with an infant, and folks accepted him. Enzo was a good father to Danny. But when he died, I have a hunch that was a big loss to the boy. That's why I called Rosalie in to see me in the hospital. That's why I tried to persuade her that, since you were back, she should tell you the truth. And I can't say I'm sorry she followed my advice…"

Bryce hadn't even suspected his father's role in Rosalie's sudden admission, and he didn't buy it now. "You think that's why Rosalie told me? Because you wanted her to?"

"Yes, of course."

Marjorie gasped. "Roland, I had no idea that's why you called Rosalie to see you that day. I would have stopped you. You had no right to put this idea into her head without talking to me first." She paused to huff an indignant breath. "Just because you all of a sudden have this urge to be a grandfather..."

"Oh, come on, Marjorie. Do you think that day was the first time Rosalie ever thought about telling Bryce the truth? You can't be that naive."

Bryce held up his hand. "Stop it, both of you. Dad may have told Rosalie to tell me the truth, but I don't think that's why she did it." He thought of the times in the last week that Rosalie had stalled when he had asked to see her, invented excuses to keep them apart. "She had a whole week to come clean about Danny after seeing Dad," he said. "And she didn't until we had a blowup outside the locker room after Danny got the wind knocked out of him in the game."

Roland looked up, startled. "He did? Is he all right?"

"Sure. It was nothing, but Rosalie acted like the sky had fallen on the kid. And she wasn't happy with my nonchalance about the whole thing. That's when the words just sort of spilled out of her mouth…with a little prodding from me."

And then a chilling realization hit him hard. "I don't know if she ever would have told me," he said, every word heavy with regret.

"I think she would have," Roland said. "But there's only one person who knows the truth of that."

"I know what you're going to say."

"Talk to her, son. Don't leave things the way they are now. A boy separated from his mother. A mother grieving over a loss again. It's not right, Bryce. Despite how you feel, and I know this is hard, you've got to swallow your pride, stand up and do what needs to be done."

As if he knew what that was!

"We have a chance to be a family now," Roland said. "Let's not waste valuable time."

Bryce closed his eyes, let his father's words filter through all the other emotions trying to claim his attention. How could he forgive Rosalie for cutting him out of their son's life? How could they go back to the way things were just one day ago? How could he advise his son about what to do when he didn't know himself? Suddenly Bryce was achingly tired. And confused. Yet still bitter. How the hell was he supposed to make any of this right when he couldn't make sense of his own thoughts?

His phone rang. He read his home phone number. And deep inside him, something flared. A small, almost unrecognizable sign of hope. A small wellspring of something good had begun to fill up the hole in his heart. He depressed the connect button. "Hey, kid. How are you?"

"Okay. I had the cereal."

"And I bet you're still hungry."

"I looked in your freezer. Do you live on frozen pizza?"

Bryce smiled. "Mostly."

"Say, Coach, I'm supposed to work at the produce stand at ten o'clock today. It's something I do for my grandmother on Saturday mornings. I can walk over there…"

Bryce checked his watch. "No, I'll take you. Be home in fifteen minutes."

"I don't want to see my mother. Just leave me at the stand."

"Whatever you want."

Bryce hung up. Maybe Danny didn't want to see his mother, but Bryce had decided Rosalie was exactly who *he* wanted to see.

Bryce had Danny at the stand five minutes early. The kid got out of the truck and immediately began removing tarps from the tables.

"Where's your grandmother?" Bryce said.

"She's probably at her church ladies' group.

She goes most every week and I don't see her car at the house."

"Your mother's car is there," Bryce said, staring up the drive.

Danny kept busy, ignoring the reference to Rosalie. He checked the cash box under the stand. "I guess there's enough change for me to get started."

"What are you going to do when your mom comes down here? You know she'll want to talk to you."

"I'm not talking to her. If she sticks around here I'll just go up to the house and get my bike and ride back to your place." He waited for Bryce to say something. When he didn't, Danny added, "That's okay with you, isn't it?"

"Sure. I've got no problem with your plan except for how it might make your mother feel."

"I hope it makes her feel as rotten as she made me feel," Danny said. "She deserves it."

Bryce couldn't figure out where his own sudden thoughts came from. As if he should have a sympathetic word for Rosalie. But he said, "Maybe, but she loves you, and that has to count for something. I don't know when I've ever seen a mother so protective of her child, so caring. Despite what she did, you have to be grateful for that."

"You call that love?" Danny said. "I call it selfishness. Now I know why she didn't want me to play football. She didn't want you and me to be together in case the truth came out."

"Okay, that might be partly true, but I think she was sincerely worried that something bad would happen to you like it did your uncle Ricky."

Danny began filling small baskets with peaches. He stopped and made finger circles at the side of his head. "It's always about Ricky, isn't it? She's always been a little nuts about what happened to that dude."

Bryce rubbed his hand over his nape. "Danny, 'that dude' was my best friend and one of the greatest guys I've ever known. When he died it was like your mom lost a part of herself."

Danny straightened, made fists at his sides. "Are you going to stand there and defend her?"

Is that what he was doing? Bryce certainly hadn't set out to defend Rosalie. And he realized now that he'd better tread carefully. Danny had been hurt badly last night. He might think of his coach as his only ally now. Bryce couldn't damage their tenuous relationship. "I'm not defending her exactly," he said. "I just think that other than this issue, she's been a pretty good mother to you."

Danny shifted into overdrive, stacking vegetables with gritty determination. "I don't want to talk about her."

Bryce raised his hands. "Fair enough. I think I'll go up and see if anyone's at the house."

"Suit yourself. But tell her not to bother coming down here. I'm doing this for my grandmother, not her."

"Okay. I'll tell her."

Assuming Danny wouldn't be opening up the stand this morning, Rosalie had dressed in jeans and an old T-shirt and made a ponytail of her hair with an ancient elastic band. She was ready to head down when she heard Bryce's truck at the end of the drive. Her heart warmed at the sight of her son getting out the passenger side. She didn't fool herself into thinking he'd forgiven her, but when he started to set up, she realized he hadn't forsaken his entire connection to his family.

From the living room window, Rosalie watched the two males talking to each other. They were too far away for her to read their facial expressions, so she could only guess what they were saying. When Bryce got back in his truck, she expected him to drive away. He didn't. He pulled behind her car and cut his engine.

Her heart hammered, a dizzying contrast to the sinking feeling in her stomach. She shook her hands to relieve a strange tingle that had traveled to all her extremities. Why was Bryce here? Was he going to further condemn her? Should she take the offensive or beg for forgiveness? One thing she knew for certain. She needed more time to prepare. And she was scared.

When Bryce stepped up to the door, Dixie dashed to the threshold and whined. Her tail beat a friendly welcome. Rosalie smoothed her hands along her jeans, tucked strands of hair that had fallen from her ponytail behind her ears and opened the door.

Bryce didn't smile. He just stared at her for a moment before saying, "I hope you feel better than you look."

"Thanks. You, too."

"I don't. I feel like crap." He jerked his thumb toward the stand. "I dropped Danny off. He said he's supposed to work for Claudia."

"I'm relieved to see that he remembered. At least there's one of us Campano women he doesn't hate."

She hoped Bryce would contradict her statement. But he only shrugged one shoulder and said, "Maybe you'd better stay away from there for a while to see how things go today."

She pressed on the screen door. "Do you want to come in?"

"Yeah, thanks." He got down on one knee and scratched Dixie behind her ear. "She looks a lot like old Belle," he said.

"Mother and daughter," Rosalie said. "It's easy to see the family resemblance." She looked away when she realized her innocent comment had a more serious meaning this morning. Is this what every conversation was going to be like? A balancing act to protect feelings, prevent innuendo?

Bryce stood. "I thought we should talk, Rosalie. In spite of what's going on between us, we have Danny to consider. He's hurting right now."

As if he needed to tell her that. She was Danny's mother. She felt his pain even though he was staying a mile away. After a few hours as a father, Bryce couldn't possibly understand the deep bond she shared with her son. She looked at the ceiling, giving herself time for a mental ten-count. Resentment was no way to start this conversation, especially when her actions were what had turned everyone's world inside out.

"As long as Danny is covering the stand, we can go in the kitchen and talk," she said. "Mom's gone so we'll be alone."

She poured Bryce a coffee and settled for orange juice for herself. She'd had way too much caffeine. "What do you want to say?" It was an open-ended question, one she might regret.

Bryce stirred sugar into his cup, set the spoon on the table. She prepared herself to be blasted by him for all of her sins. She certainly didn't expect the deep sadness in his eyes when he looked at her.

"Good God, Rosie," he said. "Why didn't you tell me you were pregnant? You knew how I felt about you." He paused, looked down at his coffee and slowly shook his head. "I asked you," he said. "That night at Cappy's Place and again at my house. I asked you about Danny's father. I gave you every chance to tell the truth."

"I know," she said, her voice a hoarse whisper.

"It's funny, but somewhere inside me I sort of suspected. I even let myself *hope.* When my mother first told me you'd come back to town with a baby, I asked her how old the kid was. The dates she gave me didn't jive. And then I checked Danny's birth date on his football form." He looked up. His eyes were moist. "Jeez, Rosalie, you've lied about his birth date all these years!"

She tried to justify her actions the way she'd justified them almost fifteen years ago. "The day he was born, I moved his birth date a few weeks later in my mind," she said, as if that cleared her of all wrongdoing. "And then I just kept putting down the incorrect information. It got to be easy. I told myself I'd tell him the truth when it mattered, when he needed a passport or went away to college. I figured I'd come up with a story by then." But she hadn't made up that lie yet, and now she wouldn't have to. She'd just have to beg her son's forgiveness for the terrible lie she'd kept for his whole life.

"Were you ever going to tell him about me?"

"Truthfully, Bryce..." She flinched at her choice of words. She'd been throwing the word *truth* around a lot lately. "If you hadn't come back to town, I wouldn't have considered it. I'd made up a story about his dad and Danny had accepted it. If he ever asked for more information about the guy, I would have come up with something. But honestly, yes, I was going to tell you last night but not the way I did." She stopped when a tear ran down her cheek. She hadn't even known she was crying. "I'm so sorry."

"Rosie, I would have come home. I would have taken care of you. We could have made it work."

"No. It wouldn't have worked. Not then." She dried her face with a napkin so she could give him a clear-eyed gaze. "I didn't love you after what happened. I couldn't marry you. I couldn't even have you in my life. You were all entwined in my mind with the day Ricky died, that horrible day and that throw. I know it was an accident. I knew it then on a rational level, but I couldn't live with that image between us. I just couldn't."

He drew a long, audible breath between his teeth. "Why didn't you talk to me? I was suffering, too."

"I know, but I couldn't. You, me and Ricky… we were like the legs of a tripod, all of us connected by the past and the present. And then one of those legs was cut off, and I completely lost my balance. I had no center anymore. Meaning became senseless. Every emotion but hurt was swept into a vacuum."

He rubbed his eyes. "Oh, that damn day. That damn throw." When he opened his eyes again, he stared directly at her. She felt his emotions in the pit of her stomach. Regret, sadness, hopelessness.

"The other day you told me you loved me," he said. "We made love. Those emotions didn't come from a vacuum, Rosie. They were real." He stopped, cleared his throat. "Or did you lie about loving me, too?"

"God, no. I do love you, Bryce. You came back to Whistler Creek and helped me heal. You brought up the past, the connection we have with Ricky and that boy out there, and you made me deal with the grief I've been suffering for so long. It has been a difficult process for me, and the irony of it all is that by accepting you back into my life I may have lost you forever. And I don't know how to even begin to make all this up to you and Danny."

He stood. "Thanks for telling me all this, Rosalie."

"Where do we go from here?"

"I don't know. I've got to learn to be a father."

She smiled. "And there is a lot I have to learn about being a mother."

"I'll talk to Danny. I'll try to get him to come home. But he can stay at my place if he wants to. I won't turn him away."

"I understand."

Bryce just stood there for a moment. And then he came around the table and slid the knuckle of his index finger gently down her cheek. "It's just so damned complicated," he said.

"Yeah."

He left without saying anything else.

Chapter Eighteen

Danny came in the house a little before noon and went directly to his room. Rosalie followed him and stood in the doorway, careful not to invade his space. He took a duffel bag from his closet floor and tossed it on his bed.

She spoke softly. "Danny, we need to talk."

He yanked the zipper open with a fierce tug, and Rosalie felt as if her heart had been ripped in two.

"Grandma's at the stand," he said. "I'm packing some clothes."

"Don't do this, honey." Her voice sounded

weak, lacking confidence. Should she try being forceful? Make demands? She was, after all, the mother. The one who had betrayed her son.

"I've got to have stuff to wear to school." He glanced down his body at an oversize T-shirt and cargo shorts she'd never seen before. Obviously he'd put on some of his father's things when he got up this morning. He opened a drawer and stuffed underwear into the duffel and followed that with two pairs of jeans and a stack of T-shirts.

She searched her brain for a safe topic. When she thought of one, she said, "Can I wash your football uniform for you?"

"The team manager does that at the field house. Mine's not that dirty anyway, just a few grass stains on the back."

If he wanted her to remember him lying on the field and how she'd been gripped with panic, he'd succeeded.

"Don't go, Danny. Give me a chance to explain."

He zipped up the bag. "Coach is waiting for

me. I'll come back tomorrow for more of my stuff."

"Let me at least drive you over," she said. Anything to have a few more minutes with her son.

"I can take my bike." He approached her at the threshold to his room and stood stubbornly until she backed away. She trailed him down the hallway to the living room.

"Danny, I'm sorry. I'm sorry I hurt you. I'm sorry I kept this from you. But you have to know that I'm not sorry I had you."

"Fine, you're sorry." He kept walking.

"Honey, it wasn't all a lie. Your father did live a long way away. I never thought he would be back in our lives. I believed I could raise you in this family and you would be happy. You have been, right? We've done pretty well together up till now…"

He looped the duffel bag over his shoulder and spun around. "Oh, yeah, we've kicked ass until last night, Mom. Until your plan for controlling my life backfired."

Her eyes welled with tears. She fought to keep them from spilling over. "What can I do, Danny? What do you want me to say?"

"I want you to tell me about my dad, my *real* dad. But it's a little late, isn't it?" His voice caught at the end of the sentence, and Rosalie sensed he was as close to tears as she was. And she ached for him. So young, so confused, so in pain. And it was all her fault.

"I'm not going to give up, Danny. I'm your mother and I love you. I'm here. I'll always be here."

He stared at the floor a moment and then pushed open the screen door and went outside. Rosalie heard the garage door open and moments later, she watched him pedaling down the drive, the duffel bag over the bike's handlebars.

The next week at school was agonizing. Rosalie made a point each day to see her son. She crossed paths with him in the hallways, ran into him as he went to the field house for practice, passed his table in the cafeteria. If he was suffering any effects from the gossip mill in Whistler Creek, Rosalie couldn't tell. If anything, from what little news she heard, the kids were viewing Danny's new gene pool discovery as a badge of honor. It was a story that apparently carried a certain amount of clout. Freshman phenom discovers coach is his dad. She was relieved that the kids in school weren't making life harder for him.

And as far as Rosalie was concerned, the adults in town could talk all they wanted. She'd been the focus of gossip before and had lived through it. She would now. So she continued to teach composition, give out homework and grade papers.

As for Bryce, the few times they had encountered each other in school, he was cordial, polite, quick to say *Good morning* or *How's it going* before continuing on his way. He treated her as he did every other faculty member with one exception. She doubted his eyes clouded with such obvious pain when he greeted everyone else. His feelings, though scrupulously masked by professionalism, were still unmistakable and Rosalie comforted herself with the knowledge he still cared. And she tortured herself with the knowledge that he was still hurting.

Of course she wondered dozens of times a day how the two males she loved were getting along in their new and untested relationship. What was it like at Bryce's house? Had he assumed the responsibilities of a parent—guiding, advising, disciplining? Did they talk about her, and if they did, was there ever a kind word? Bryce said he'd try to get Danny to come home, but that hadn't happened yet. Would it ever? Or would the house Rosalie lived in always feel this lonely, as if even the wood and bricks knew its heartbeat was gone.

Was Danny still calling his father "Coach," and did either one of them miss her, even once in a while?

Rosalie filled her evening hours preparing lessons, and working extra at the Brighter Day Center. If she couldn't help herself, she could still help others. Her experience with Bryce had taught her a valuable lesson. The empty feelings of grief that seemed to stretch for an eternity could and would be overcome with other emotions in time.

She also found comfort in seeing her mother's relationship with Gordon Capps grow stronger each day. Claudia had loved Enzo; her feelings for Gordon were just as strong, but in a different way. With Cappy, Claudia experienced a freedom she had never known in her marriage, and her very spirit seemed to have taken on wings.

Which is why Rosalie wasn't surprised when her mother announced on Thursday afternoon that she was having some people over for a get-together.

"That's great," Rosalie said. "I'll plan to be out of the house. I can go to the library or…"

"Nonsense," Claudia said. "I want you here. You need to socialize."

"No, Mom, not really. I'd rather…"

"I want you here, dear. I insist."

When Claudia insisted, that was pretty much it. Rosalie figured she could greet her mother's guests, *socialize* an acceptable amount of time, and then go to her room.

Claudia prepared lasagna, fresh baked bread, salad and appetizers. Just before seven o'clock, she instructed Rosalie. "I have to run a quick errand. You and Gordon will stay and greet our guests until I get back."

"Where are you going?" Rosalie asked. "Is this something I can do for you?"

"No, no. I've got everything planned. Just keep the lasagna on warm and put out the appetizers."

Rosalie agreed though her instincts went on alert. She couldn't imagine her mother leaving for an errand at the last minute. And when the first guests knocked and Rosalie opened the door to Marjorie and Roland Benton, she was even more confused.

Danny and Bryce trudged into his house at 6:30 p.m. after an especially long team meeting and brief workout. Tomorrow night's game promised to be a challenge, and Bryce had taken extra time to prepare his guys.

He dropped his keys on an end table and stretched his back muscles. "If it's okay with you, I'll hit the shower first," he said to Danny.

He came out twenty minutes later wearing shorts and an old Dallas Cowboys T-shirt, his usual attire for taking it easy, warming up a pizza and watching TV. The pie had been in the oven ten minutes when a car pulled up his lane. Bryce stepped out onto his porch.

"Who is it, Coach?" Danny called from the living room.

"It's your grandmother."

Danny was by his side in seconds. "Grandma? Do you think something happened to Mom?"

Bryce held his breath. Yes, that had been his first thought, too. He put a reassuring hand on Danny's shoulder. "I guess we'll find out."

Claudia slammed her car door and marched up to the porch. "I made lasagna. I want you both to come over and have some."

The two males stared at Claudia before passing puzzled looks at each other. "Just us?" Bryce said.

"It's lasagna," Claudia said as if that should satisfy his curiosity. She came up on the porch, sniffed the air. "Who stinks?"

"Not me," Bryce said.

She jerked her thumb in her grandson's direction. "Go shower. You're not eating my specialty smelling like that."

Danny glanced at his father. Bryce shrugged. "Do you like her lasagna?" he asked.

"It's the greatest."

Bryce nodded. "That's the way I remember it. Then hit the head. And turn off the oven while you're in there."

"Who else is at the house?" Danny asked.

"Gordon," Claudia answered and pinched her lips into a thin line. She didn't add another name.

"Okay. Give me ten minutes."

Once Danny had left, Bryce said, "Mrs. C, I

can drive my truck over. And you could have called. You didn't have to come here."

"Personal invitations, face-to-face. Always the best."

"Well, you can leave now if you want. We'll be there as soon as Danny showers."

She plopped down on a rocking chair Bryce had purchased from the Cracker Barrel. "I'll wait. I like these chairs. I've never seen the view from your front porch. Then I'll follow you over."

"Well, thanks." He wanted to add "I think," but kept the sarcastic comment to himself. He sat on the other rocker and set it to pitching at a slow pace while they waited. No doubt, Mrs. C was acting strange.

Claudia rubbed her hands together, eliminating a telltale dampness. Gordon told her she could do this. He believed in her. She didn't want to disappoint him, or herself. Too much depended on this plan and her giving everyone a piece of her mind.

* * *

Rosalie was grateful when the front door opened. She'd been having a difficult time staying attentive to the stilted conversation with the Bentons.

"Look who I found," Claudia said, holding the door for Bryce and Danny.

Oh, wonderful. What had her mother done? This wasn't going to make conversation flow any more smoothly.

Bryce stood in the middle of the room staring at his parents. "Mom, Dad, Mrs. C didn't say you would be here." He then focused on Rosalie. "In fact, she didn't tell me about most of the guest list."

"Makes two of us," Rosalie said. Realizing they'd all been the target of her mother's manipulations, she mustered her resolve not to flee the room. She couldn't take much more plastic-coated politeness from Bryce or outright condemnation from Danny.

"Three of us," Danny added. He leaned against the door frame, his face sullen.

Claudia breezed across the room to a buffet against the far wall. "Oh, good, Rosalie. You put out the appetizers. Dinner won't be for a while so help yourselves."

"We have been, Mom," Rosalie said.

"Everything is delicious," Roland said.

Marjorie's assortment of cheese and crackers remained in a napkin on her lap, small nibbles taken from each.

No one spoke for an eternal amount of time, perhaps a minute of agony, as Claudia bustled around her trays and glassware. Finally Rosalie said, "Mom, what's going on? What are you doing?"

Claudia sighed deeply, threaded her hands at her waist and looked at Cappy. He nodded at her. She cleared her throat.

"All of you in this room mean a great deal to me," she said, her voice trembling with what seemed to be an acute attack of nerves. "Some of you, I have loved for years. One of you I've come to love for only a short time."

Cappy smiled. Rosalie did, as well. Love! Imagine that.

"Some of you have just recently become important to me," Claudia continued. She pressed the tips of her thumbs together, breathed in. "But frankly, a few of you are acting like the ass end of a horse."

Rosalie almost choked. That was as close to hearing an inappropriate expression from her mother as she could remember. Claudia's cheeks reddened. Rosalie stood up and took a step toward her.

Cappy put up his hand, gesturing for Rosalie to sit back down. "Leave her alone. She's fine."

"Thank you, Gordon," Claudia said. "Now then, I want to tell a story."

Everyone waited without saying a word.

"I was married to a fine man. Enzo was a good husband. He took care of his family. He was kind to me and his children. But he was a man who believed in the old ways, the ways of his father. He made certain rules in his household and I obeyed them." She smiled at Rosalie.

"Sometimes his children did not. But I always did. I was respectful to Enzo, tried always to please him. An example of this would be my appearance. I never wore pants outside the house. I did not cut my hair short.

"After Enzo died, I must admit to experiencing a certain lightness with the lessening of restraints. It took me a while, but eventually I wore slacks, even to church." Her voice took on a steely edge of strength when she said, "And I went to the beauty salon and got my hair cut."

"Mom, you look beautiful, but I don't see…"

"Let me finish, Rosalie. You will understand everything." She dropped her arms to her sides and made loose fists of her hands. "I brought you here tonight to tell you that you all need haircuts."

Roland chuckled. Danny, whose hair was most always in his eyes, flashed his grandmother a confused stare. "What are you talking about, Grandma?"

"In everyone's life, important things happen, life-changing things. We can hide from them or we can face them straight on. So we must decide if we are going to let our hair grow over our eyes or if we are going to cut it off so we can see. Such a life-changing thing has happened to all of us in recent days."

She narrowed her eyes at Marjorie. "Mrs. Benton…Marjorie…you already have a fine son. But your life could be even better if you got to know your grandson. And you could discover a dear friend in Rosalie Campano. You have only to look at these two and really see them.

"Roland, you have a second chance at life which can bring you great pleasure. You can bring these people into the arms of your family." She nodded gently at him. "I think you are the most ready of anyone in this room to do that."

"Yes, I am," he said.

"Bryce…"

He slowly lowered himself onto the sofa. His eyes widened as he waited for his message.

"…in the seven weeks you have been home,

you have started a new job, bought a house and found a son. If that isn't a reason for a haircut, I don't know what is. You need to look at the gifts you have been given, no matter how you came to get them. You have been blessed, Bryce Benton, not cursed."

When her mother turned her attention to her, Rosalie straightened her back and held her breath for the onslaught. She wasn't ready to bear the brunt of everyone's problems, but was determined to at least accept the criticism with grace.

"Rosalie," Claudia began, "it is time for you to stop apologizing to everyone. You made a mistake, you admitted it, now stop begging for everyone's forgiveness."

What? This wasn't at all what Rosalie expected. She slowly released the air from her lungs.

"The truth has not diminished you," Claudia said. "It has made you taller, stronger, a better person. It is past time for you to realize that whatever the future holds, you can face it with the knowledge that you have now done the right thing and there is no more you can do."

The first wet, sloppy tear slid down Rosalie's cheek. She wiped it away, stole a look at Bryce. Even through the swampy blur of her eyes, he was the light and the clarity of her life.

"And Danny," Claudia said. "Our greatest blessing. You came to us when we needed you most. Do not throw away the gifts that God has given you. A grandmother who loves you, new grandparents who will take you into their lives, a father who is ready to get to know you and guide you. And a mother who has sacrificed to give you a happy life and who only wants to see you enrich that life now."

Claudia sniffed, bit her lower lip. "Your haircut is easy, Danny. All you have to do is brush away the bitterness and forgive."

Claudia took a deep breath, one that seemed to catch in her chest. But she found the will to continue. "I've said what I have to say. Except that we can be a family. One with flaws, yes.

One that makes mistakes, certainly. But one that can learn and love and move forward. It's what I want, what I pray for every night." She covered her mouth and coughed. "Now it's up to you. I have made the lasagna. I ask you to come to my table and share it together."

Cappy stood, went to Claudia and gave her a hug. The room was silent, as if each person were deep in his own thoughts. Finally Bryce looked at Rosalie, smiled and said, "I don't know about the rest of you, but I'm starving and that lasagna smells awful good."

"Beats frozen pizza," Danny said.

And seven people sat around the Campano kitchen table and had dinner. And talked about anything and everything, but mostly what they had in common, the Campanos and the Bentons.

After dinner, Rosalie rinsed the dishes and put them in the dishwasher. Through the window she watched her family and guests on the back patio. She was encouraged that Claudia's gathering hadn't broken up when the last piece of lasagna had been served. Rosalie had no idea what tomorrow would bring, but tonight she realized she would get through this heartache. She would have her son back. She'd have to share him, but he had begun to forgive her.

Bryce? She didn't know. He had talked to her during dinner. His polite exterior was gone, replaced by a more natural, friendly demeanor. They had bantered back and forth about their past. It was almost like the old days. And even a little like the last few weeks.

Finished with her chore, Rosalie went into the bathroom, saw her reflection in the mirror and did some repair to her face. She hid the circles under her eyes with concealer, added a bit of blush and powdered the shine off her nose. Probably a waste of effort, she thought, leaving the bathroom. She'd started down the hallway when a strong hand grabbed her arm and propelled her through the living room to the front door.

Before she could speak, she was outside, alone on the darkened porch with Bryce. When she caught her breath, she said, "Don't you ever get tired of abducting women from bathrooms?"

"I'm more selective now," he said. "I don't grab any woman who has a purse she can use as a weapon."

She smiled. And almost cried. "You coaches aren't as thickheaded as people say."

He led her to the swing hanging from the porch ceiling and sat beside her. "I don't know. I can be at times."

She curled her legs under her and let him set the swing in motion. It felt wonderful not to have to do a thing, not even control the swing. She was so tired of trying to be strong.

After a moment he turned to her and said, "So where do we go from here, Rosalie?"

"I think that's your decision."

"Really?" He rubbed the nape of his neck.

"We have a son, you know. Shouldn't all of our decisions be mutual?"

"About him, yes."

He grinned. "I got you to say yes to that. I'm quite an arbitrator."

"Well, he is your son, too. And I can see he's happy about that."

"He hasn't called me 'Dad' yet."

"Have you asked him to?"

"I will in time."

He continued to rock the swing. The old metal hinge above their heads squeaked, a normal, comfortable summer sound. On the other side of the porch rail, crickets made their nightly calls, burrowing animals dug among the roots of the magnolia trees. The scents of Claudia's flowers swirled around them, heady and sweet.

And as natural as the warmth of a September Georgia night, Rosalie laid her head on Bryce's shoulder. The hinge stopped squeaking. She turned to look up at him and met eyes filled with hope and promise and love.

"Ah, Rosie-girl, how did it all go so wrong?"

he said. "And how lucky are we to have a second chance now?"

He bent his head and kissed her. And when Rosalie's mind cleared from the sheer joy of his kiss, she thought of what Roland Benton had said. They had come full circle and nothing had ever felt so right.

"From this day on," he said. "We share in *all things Danny,* okay?"

"Okay."

"And when other kids come…"

She inhaled a sharp breath. "What?"

"Are you opposed to having more? Maybe two?"

"I love kids, but I'm not prepared to go about it the same way I did before."

"You mean not with me?"

"I didn't say that."

"I'm not going anywhere, Rosie. I'm staying in Whistler Creek. Hell and high water couldn't drive me away."

She smiled, nestled closer in his arms.

"But you're going somewhere," he said.

HIS MOST IMPORTANT WIN

"I am?"

"Yeah. I'm going to try and persuade you to move a mile down the road, toward the old mill, the Harbin place to be exact. It's been fixed up pretty nice."

"It has, hasn't it?" She grinned. "But why would I do that?"

"Because that's where your husband will be. And hopefully our son. And Dixie if you want her to come. You can go with a clear conscience because I have a hunch Claudia won't need you anymore in this house."

"I have a hunch you're right."

"Tomorrow's another day, Rosie. And I'm ready to face it with you."

She reached her arms around his neck and kissed him with all the love that was close to bursting from her chest. Who would have thought it could end like this.

* * * * *

WEB_M&B_RTL3 LP

Discover Pure Reading Pleasure with

Visit the Mills & Boon website for all the latest in romance

Buy all the latest releases, backlist and eBooks

Find out more about our authors and their books

Join our community and chat to authors and other readers

Free online reads from your favourite authors

Win with our fantastic online competitions

Sign up for our free monthly eNewsletter

Tell us what you think by signing up to our reader panel

Rate and review books with our star system

www.millsandboon.co.uk

 Follow us at twitter.com/millsandboonuk

 Become a fan at facebook.com/romancehq